TOM'S RIDE

A MORGAN'S RUN ROMANCE

M. LEE PRESCOTT

Tom's Ride

By

M. Lee Prescott

Published by Mt. Hope Press
Copyright 2022, M. Lee Prescott
ISBN: 978-1-7379034-0-6

Cover Design by Ashley Lopez
Front cover image: *depositphotos.com/alanpoulson*
Back Cover Image: *jasonyoo/bigstock.com*

http://www.mleeprescott.com/

This book is dedicated to the health workers, essential workers, and all who have courageously given of themselves to keep us safe and healthy during the past two years.

WHO'S WHO IN MORGAN'S RUN

BOOKS 1-12

Dear Readers,
As this series continues, the cast of characters continues to grow. To celebrate book 12, I've included the "Who's Who" below so that you can keep up with everyone.
Enjoy!
ML

Morgan's Run

Ben and Leonora Morgan, owners of Morgan's Run Ranch, Inn and Spa, also Valley Stables, a thoroughbred farm with Spark Foster

- **Ben Morgan,** manages the ranch, married to Maggie Williams, two children, Emma and Ben
- **Sam Morgan,** architect, married to Rose Dillon
- **Beth Morgan,** runs the ranch's farm with Ruthie Morgan, married to Lang Dillon, daughter, **Lily** and son, **Tucker**
- **Robbie Morgan,** runs an adventure tours company, married to **Hope Seymour,** artist
- **Kyle Morgan,** veterinarian, married to Harriet Winthrop, a teacher

- **Ruthie Morgan,** runs the ranch's farm with Beth Morgan, married to Harley Langdon, two daughters, **Willow, Charlotte and Penelope "Pickles"**
- **Carmela Rodriquez,** cook/housekeeper, married to **Raoul,** ranch livestock manager
- **Harley Langdon,** manages the ranch's stables, married to Ruthie Morgan, three daughters, **Willow, Charlotte** and **Penelope "Pickles"**
- **Maggie Williams,** Harley's assistant manager and trainer
- **Jeb Barnes,** Maggie's assistant trainer, married to Amy Foster, one child, Toby
- **Nick Parker,** horse whisper/trainer
- **Brendan Stadler,** stable hand Morgan's Run Stables

Lodge and Spa

- **Jim Thompson,** manager
- **Bebe Corcoran, assistant manager**
- **George Baran,** head chef
- **Mel Farrell,** manages the Spa, married to Rita Lazares, yoga teacher

Emma's Dream, summer camp on the ranch, started by Maggie and Ben Morgan

- **Johnny Stockdale,** cook

Cottage Day Care, built by Spark Foster and Ben and Leonora Morgan to provide care for the ranch's children

- **Lynn Manguelli,** co-director, married to Gus Casey
- **Polly Granger,** co-director, married to Kevin Larrabee

Visitors

- **Helen Winthrop**, friend of Leonora from New England, becomes a close companion to Spark Foster
- **Harriet Winthrop**, Helen's daughter, marries Kyle Morgan

Spark Foster's Estate

Spark Foster, owner of Foster Enterprises, an engineering firm specializing in alternative energy. Also co-owns Valley Stables, a thoroughbred farm with Ben Morgan Senior

- **Buck Foster**, Spark's son, lives in Laguna Beach, California
- **Amy Foster**, married to **Jeb Barnes**, one child, **Toby**
- **Aria Firorelli**, Spark's personal chef
- **Mickey Collins**, Spark's pilot
- **Jimmy-Halliday**, Spark's driver
- **Fred Butler**, Spark's Portland-based attorney
- **Kevin Larrabee**, Spark's contractor, married to Polly Granger

Saguaro Valley Winery

Jay and Martha Dillon, owners, two children

- **Lang Dillon**, married to Beth Morgan, owns Rambler Sports West, daughter **Lily** and son, **Tucker**
- **Rose Dillon**, married to Sam Morgan
- **Neecy Rodriquez**, housekeeper, married to **Manuel "Manny" Rodriquez**, winery manager
- **Roger Faircloth**, vintner
- **Jon Wilson**, Dillon's personal chef

Valley Stables
A thoroughbred farm owned by Ben Morgan Senior and Spark Foster

- **Harley Langdon,** manager after leaving his job at Morgan's Run stables
- **Tom Jacobi,** assistant manager, head trainer
- **Bella Jacobi,** Tom's sister and local midwife
- **Gus Casey,** head trainer until he moves east
- **Greg Patterson,** wrangler, ranch hand
- **William "Whip" Kittredge,** wrangler/hand
- **Greg Patterson,** wrangler/hand
- **Kyle Morgan,** resident veterinarian until he moves east with Harriet
- **Patty Turner,** assistant to Kyle, then takes over as resident veterinarian when Kyle moves east

Town of Saguaro Valley

- **Ned Williams,** Maggie's dad, lives in town, assists ranches as a veterinarian
- **Gracie Walker,** owns Gracie's Diner
- **Haley Alvarez,** therapist
- **Russ Keelor, owns the Bulldog Saloon**
- **Gabriella Huff,** owns Gabriela's, a dress shop
- **Wrenn Parsons,** acupuncturist, dating Ned Williams
- **Dara Littlefield,** Maggie's best friend from high school
- **Edna and Oscar Loggins,** owners of Vermillion, a popular farm-to-table south of town
- **Wilbur McGraw, owns Valley Hardware**
- **Grace McGraw,** Wilbur's daughter
- **Chester Black,** town physician

CHAPTER 1

"Come on, Boss, a night on the town won't kill you," Whip Kitteridge said as he and Tom Jacobi walked side by side, each leading a thoroughbred into the stables for the night.

Tom gave the wrangler a crooked smile, shaking his head. "Hanging out with your lot just might kill me. Besides, I'm in the middle of a great book."

The handsome cowboy with shoulder-length, dirty-blond hair, beard, and mustache stopped in his tracks, one eyebrow raised. "Book? On a Saturday night? You've got to be kidding."

"Nope. Reading a terrific mystery by—"

"Stop right there. Don't know, don't wanna know. You're coming with us. Period, end of story. It's Greg's birthday, and he'll be bummed if you don't show."

Tom was pretty sure Greg wouldn't notice if he was there or not, but what the hell? He could pick up with Roger Demaris and his team tomorrow. Tom had never been back east, but he loved reading regional series set in New England. In this book, *A Friend of Silence,* he found that he identified with the main character, a flawed, angry man who was trying to change his outlook on the world.

"Fine, but I'll meet you there."

Whip pumped a fist in the air. "Yes! We're leavin' for the Bulldog at seven. We'll come by your house and lay on the horn so you'll know when to hightail it into town."

Good thing we live out here in the middle of nowhere, Tom thought, leading Blue into his stall.

"Okay, boy, all set. Lucky you, getting to call it a night," Tom said, stroking the magnificent animal's muzzle.

The tall chestnut Trakehner was one of four purchased by Valley Stables for their dressage program. Blue no longer competed, but had been acquired for stud. Spirited and proud, Trakehners were valued for the purity of their line, but were also bred with other horses as refiners.

As Blue was the last horse into the barn most nights, Tom always spent more time with him. Wranglers and stable managers tried to avoid having favorites, but Tom had loved Blue from the moment he laid eyes on him. His own horse, Buckles, had died shortly after he moved to Saguaro Valley of a rare fever complicated by laminitis, and he still missed him. He was looking for a new horse, but for now, whenever he wanted to ride, there were plenty of horses at Valley Stables. Tom almost always rode Blue.

After closing up the barn, he walked the short distance back to his place, the beautiful farmhouse he'd inherited from the former assistant trainer, Gus Casey. Gus had moved east to be near his wife's family and now worked for Tom's boss's brother, Richard Morgan, at the sprawling five-hundred-acre farm, Morgan's Fire. Tom breathed in the cool valley air, thinking how fortunate he was to land in the little slice of heaven that was Saguaro Valley. An unusual cloud formation and the accompanying moisture had created this extraordinary green valley in between two mountain ranges, with mountains and desert surrounding it. An orographic effect, it was called.

Since their college days, his bosses, Ben Morgan and his best friend, Spark Foster, had dreamed of opening stables training thoroughbreds and now, their dream had been realized. Like everything the two men touched, Valley Stables was wildly successful. In its second year, the ranch was beginning to receive national and international attention, both for the quality of its stock and for the wild horses rescue program. The latter expanded the already-established rescue efforts based at Ben's home ranch, Morgan's Run. Tom had been hired as assistant manager by Harley Langdon, his boss's son-in-law. He divided his working day between the thoroughbred stables and training facility and the wild horses "down the hill." He and Harley had hired good people, including Whip, and their efforts had contributed in no small way to Valley Stables' success.

After showering, Tom grabbed a beer and came to sit on the back porch, waiting for the crew. As he leaned back in a porch rocker, his cell phone rang. His sister, Bella.

"Hey, Bella, what's up?"

"I got the offer today."

"For?"

"For Valley OB-GYN. They want me to start next week."

"You're kidding."

"No... I told you I was applying."

"I know, but I thought it was just one of your spur-of-the-moment, crazy ideas."

"Ha-ha."

"You love Missoula," he said, scratching his head as he gazed out at the mountains. Before his move to Saguaro Valley, Tom had lived in the Flathead Valley northwest of Missoula, Montana. His sister was the only thing he missed about Montana. Beautiful country, but too much heartache.

"Not anymore. With Mom and Dad *and* my big brother gone, I'm ready to make a change. I'll be one of a group of three midwives. Slightly smaller practice, but it's gonna be great."

Two trucks pulled into the drive, horns blaring. "What's that noise?" Bella asked.

Tom waved the men onward, pointing to the phone in his hand. More honking and shouting as they drove away. "My crazy crew. They're headed for a birthday party in town."

"Can't wait to meet them!"

The cowboy factor, he thought. *I'll have to watch those guys around my sister.* "So...wow sis, you're full of surprises."

"Very funny. Surprises? You and I have been talking about this for three months. Now, have you done your research? What leads have you gotten on apartments, condos, whatever down there?"

"You're moving in with me. This is a huge house, and I'd be happy for the company."

"Well, maybe temporarily. That would be great actually, if you're sure? I'm selling or giving away a bunch of stuff and will bring a small U-Haul load down. Any storage places nearby?"

"A big empty barn right behind my house."

Silence. Finally she said, "You're pleased about this, right? We're all that we have left of family."

"Course I'm pleased. Do you need help moving at your end?"

"No, thanks. Derrick has volunteered. It's the least he can do. I'll suck it up for the couple of hours it takes to load the truck." Derrick was her longtime boyfriend, who had recently broken things off with no explanation.

Tom had never liked Derrick Slocum, Bella's partner since grad school. "Why don't you let me hire a local mover so you don't have to interact with that scumbag."

"It will be fine. A couple of hours Friday afternoon, and I'll be rid of him for good."

"Alright, if you're sure. So when are you headed this way?"

"Saturday morning. I'm taking three days. Should be in Saguaro by Monday night, if things go as planned."

"I thought you said they wanted you next week?"

"I start Wednesday. You okay? You sound a little down."

"Nah, you know me. Laconic cowboy."

"Can't wait to see you, big brother."

"Me too."

They talked awhile longer, then Tom rang off, thinking again how much he'd rather stay home. Finally succumbing to the inevitable, he went inside, tossed his empty beer bottle and grabbed a jacket from the mudroom.

CHAPTER 2

When Tom arrived at the Bulldog, Greg Patterson's party was already in full swing. The gang from Valley Stables had taken over the saloon's side room behind the bar, and tables were covered with empty shot glasses, beer bottles, and half-eaten plates of food. Tom nodded at the owner, Russ Keeler, who was delivering heaping plates of food to a booth in the back. He waited until the short, burly man with flaming red hair, a ruddy complexion, and warm, twinkling blue eyes returned to his post behind the bar.

"Hey, Russ, the guys aren't getting out of hand, are they?"

"Not yet. Harley's in the corner babysitting, and the big bosses are having dinner back there." He gestured toward a booth as far from the raucous birthday crowd as possible.

Tom laughed, turning to spy Ben Morgan Senior and Spark Foster, then to the side room where his boss, Harley Langdon, sat at a table chatting with his best friend, Ben Senior's oldest, also named Ben, and Patty Turner, Valley Stables' resident veterinarian. "I'm sure Harley's thrilled to be here with a two-year-old and a very pregnant wife at home. I'll take over in a while."

"What can I get you?"

"Desert Amber draft would be great, thanks."

Tom took his beer and strolled through his men, who were sitting and standing around the room in various states of intoxication. *They move fast*, he thought, shaking his head. Since Whip acted three sheets to the wind even when sober, it was hard to gauge where he was on the drunkenness spectrum. His loud, raucous voice rose above his companions' as they urged Greg to down a shot of tequila followed by a beer chaser.

"Hey, Kitteridge," Tom said as he passed by the group of wranglers. "Go easy. We've got a full day tomorrow, and I need these guys in good shape." They were expecting five wild horses, and settling them in would require all wranglers to be sober and alert. They were also bringing their new jockeys in for time trials with a couple of the thoroughbreds.

Whip waved over his shoulder. "No worries, boss. I'm watchin' out for them."

Yeah, watchin' out as they fall over a cliff, Tom thought, shaking his head. *Clearly, the birthday boy will be useless tomorrow.* Tom decided to give them an hour, then send them back to the bunkhouses. He reached Harley and his companions, pulled up a chair and gazed from one to the other. "Hey, how's it going?"

Patty rolled her eyes. "About as well as expected with this group of bozos. They're idiots, the whole lot of them."

Tom looked at his boss, who had a huge grin on his face, green eyes lit up. "I can think of many nights this one," Harley said, gesturing to his best friend, "and me looked worse than that."

"Guilty as charged," Ben said, leaning back in his chair, chuckling. "Geez, check out Patterson. Looks like he's about to lose the Bulldog Burger he just scarfed down." Since coming home and marrying Maggie Williams, Ben had taken over most of the management of his family's ranch, Morgan's Run. Dark haired and dark eyed, he had the Morgan smile that made women go weak at the knees.

"Think we should yank 'em now?" Harley asked. Stetson beside him on the table, his sandy hair had a serious case of hat head, but it didn't matter. The drop-dead gorgeous cowboy turned women's heads wherever he went. Now happily married to Ruthie Morgan, youngest child of Ben and Leonora Morgan, fatherhood had curtailed his and

Ben's earlier exploits, but they still enjoyed a good party now and then.

"Give 'em an hour and I'll round 'em up," Tom said, turning to Ben. "Where's the beautiful Ms. Morgan tonight?"

Ben grinned. "Not her scene. Her days of hanging out with drunken wranglers are over. Took the kids to the movies."

"She's pregnant, I hear," Tom said.

"Yup, a regular Valley baby boom, what with her and Ruthie and who knows who else. Our mom's apoplectic thinking about all the babies coming, and she's just recovering from her second hip surgery."

"If she's anything like my mom, she'll be fit as a fiddle before any of your babies arrive. My mom was riding and jogging a month after she had her hip replaced," Tom said.

"Let's hope so. Thank God they built the Cottage. What would we all do about child care without it?" Harley said, referring to the day care and nursery the elder Morgans and Spark had built on Morgan's Run. The inviting state-of-the-art space was open and free to all the employees working at Morgan's Run and Valley Stables.

An hour later, Whip, Greg, and all their friends had been hustled out and taken back to the stables, fifteen miles north of town. Ben and Harley had taken a couple and Patty had loaded others too drunk to drive into one of the Valley Stables vans. Tom confiscated their keys and was planning to drive Whip and a few stranglers back when he realized that his head wrangler was perfectly sober and could take the rest of the gang in his truck.

"Hey, Whip, drive safe and make sure these guys hit the hay soon. We have a long, hard day tomorrow."

"Yeah, boss, no prob," Whip said, tipping his hat.

Tom headed back into the bar, passing the familiar black-and-white photos of Valley rodeo stars. Ned Williams, father to Maggie, Ben's wife, was featured in many photos. The most famous wrangler to come out of the area, he was second to none, with Harley right behind him. He found Russ and checked to make certain everyone had settled their tabs. As the two men chatted, Russ seemed distracted, his gaze focused on something behind him. "Everything okay?" Tom asked.

Russ shook his head. "Poor kid. She shouldn't have to deal with this every goddamn night."

Tom turned to spy Wilbur McGraw, owner of Valley Hardware, with his arm over his daughter's shoulder, leaning heavily against her. As the men watched, McGraw did a nose dive onto the table of an empty booth.

"Geez," Tom said. "I've got this. Russ." He rushed to the booth and lifted the now comatose man from the bar. "Hey, Wilbur, time to go home."

"It's okay," she said softly. "If he rests a minute, I can manage."

"No problem Grace. Where's your ride?" Tom didn't know her well, but even in her harried state, Grace McGraw was beautiful. A wisp of a thing, her straight, shoulder-length sandy hair was in a scraggly ponytail, no doubt disarranged by her struggle. She wore jeans and a pale green sweatshirt, Valley Hardware splayed across the front. She had a kind of beauty that touched his heart. More than once, he'd thought of asking her out when he'd shopped at the hardware store, but had always chickened out.

Her lovely hazel eyes met his, her distress evident. "That's part of the problem. We walked. We're just a couple of blocks away, behind the store."

"Well then, we'll take my truck. I'm Tom. I work at Valley Stables."

"Yes," she said softly as they made their way to the door.

Tom called, "Night, Russ," nodding to the owner.

"Good luck," Russ said before turning to his customers at the crowded bar.

After wrestling Wilbur McGraw into the truck's front seat, Grace squeezed in beside him. "Fortunately it's a short drive," she said.

As they reached the hardware store, she said, "If you drive around to the back of the lot, our driveway's right there."

Tom pulled up alongside the white farmhouse, shrouded in darkness, and Grace jumped out. "I'll run in and turn on some lights."

As he waited, several windows lit up, and then the porch light. By the time she reached the truck, Tom had her father over his shoulder. "You lead the way. I've got him."

He stepped through the door and gazed around at the neat, simply furnished parlor with a sofa covered in blue-and-white calico, two easy chairs covered in faded denim, and a green leather recliner set three feet from the television. Bookshelves and a variety of small tables completed the décor along with a wood stove adjacent to the stairway leading up to the second floor.

"Do you mind bringing him back here? His bedroom's just down the hall," she said.

"Of course not."

She led him past the kitchen and dining room to an open door down the hallway. She reached around and switched on an overhead light to a small room just large enough for a double bed and chest of drawers. "This is the guest room, but since my mom died he refuses to sleep upstairs in their bedroom. Just dump him on the bed, thanks."

Tom lay Wilbur down as best he could. Grace pulled off his boots and threw a patchwork quilt over him. "That's good. He'll sleep it off and have forgotten all about it in the morning."

As they stepped out of the room, she switched off the light and closed the door. When they stood in the parlor again, she said, "Thank you so much. I'm sorry you had to go out of your way. It's embarrassing, frustrating, and difficult, but that's Dad. After my mother died last year, he fell apart. We just went out for burgers, but somehow he manages to drink himself under the table by dessert no matter how hard I try to stop him."

"Big burden for you," Tom said, gazing down at her lovely face, her eyes rimmed with tears. "Are there any other family members to help you?"

She shook her head. "There's my Aunt Gracie, but she's busy with the diner. I have a brother and two sisters, but they don't live here. One of my sisters comes every so often to give me a break, but the others are caught up in their own lives. Would you like some coffee or hot chocolate before you go? It's the least I can do."

"Ordinarily, I'd accept with pleasure," he said, watching the light play in her hazel eyes. "But we have a big day at the stables tomorrow. Work'll be starting in a few hours. Maybe a rain check?"

She smiled, a warm delightful smile that smoothed away her distress for a few seconds. "I'd like that."

"I come into the hardware store from time to time, but I've only caught glimpses of you."

"I've seen you," she said, hand on her hip, "but I spend a lot of time in the office out in back."

Tom grinned. "I should have snooped around. Next time, I'll be nosier. Maybe someday if things are slow, I could take you out for coffee?"

"That sounds nice," she said as he opened the door.

"Well, good night." He smiled, then turned away.

"Night."

As Grace watched the handsome, lanky cowboy head to his truck, her heart ached with loneliness. Thinking about his kindness, given so freely and unselfishly, brought tears to her eyes. She waved as he backed out, then closed the door. *How I wish I could've gone with you, Tom Jacobi. Anywhere to escape this.*

CHAPTER 3

Saturday morning at seven, the huge trailer carrying five new mustangs arrived. They wanted to get the horses settled before the day's main activities, time trials for several of the thoroughbreds, the first time their new jockey, Rupert, would be participating. They had thoroughbred horses coming from ranches and stables as far away as Albuquerque and many towns north and west of the Valley. A couple of noncontenders from Morgan's Run were also participating to round out the field.

Tom saddled Blue and rode down to the lower barn. He and Harley had been working on the logistics of the time trials for weeks. He shook his head, watching a couple of his wranglers, clearly hungover, as they headed toward the trailer. *Birthday parties*, he thought. *I'll have to keep some of these dopes down here out of sight. Can't have them hobnobbing with the hoi polloi up the hill.*

Dangerous work that could get a man killed with one fall or stumble, it was hell to transfer wild horses from trailers to paddocks. Hungover cowboys had no place near wild horses starving and just off the range.

"Kittridge!" Tom yelled, spying his wrangler. "Send Patterson and anyone else who looks like shit to help muck out the stalls. We don't need them underfoot."

Whip nodded. "Sure, boss, right away."

"And don't let them near Harley unless they want to get skinned alive."

"You got it."

"And get the rest of the guys down here pronto."

Just as Whip disappeared, Harley drove up in his truck, hanging his head out the window. "You okay down here?"

"Yup. Guys are coming right now."

"I'll be up at the stables getting Stella and Leo ready and making sure the guest stalls are all set. Phone if you need more help. I grabbed up all the part-timers to work up there, but maybe we can spare a couple?"

"We got this, boss. No worries."

As Harley drove off, crossing the short distance to the stables, Tom shook his head again. *We got this, yeah right*, he thought. *Bunch of idiots.*

When Tom met the team, finally assembled, the sounds of whinnying, clattering hooves, and loud snorts came from the long trailer with its five terrified horses inside. "Okay, Eddie," he called to the driver. "Back her up slow now."

Eddie backed up until the rear of the long trailer was at the open gate of the largest paddock. Two of the men held the gate against the trailer's side, blocking the part of the opening that was slightly wider than the trailer's back door. The horses were each in their own stall and would be released one at a time. As Whip slid open the door, a pure white stallion reared, hooves flying, then bolted into the open corral, pawing, stamping, and throwing back his massive white head. Whip watched, pushing back his Stetson and scratching his forehead. "Wow, he's a beauty and looks pretty healthy. Does he play well with others?"

"No," Tom said. "According to the park service, he's in the best shape of this lot, but not very friendly. Watch yourself, now. You can let the second one out. If there's any trouble, we'll move the stallion to the far paddock."

"That'll be interesting getting a rope around that neck," Whip said.

The batch of mustangs had all been part of the same herd, so they had decided to try them together and separate later if necessary. The second horse, pied colored and at least four hands shorter than the stallion, resembled an American Paint. He skittered out, giving the stallion a wide berth. His ribs were visible, his coat matted and caked with mud.

"Poor guy," Whip said as they watched the wary, frightened creature.

The next two were mares in similar condition to the Paint. Both about fifteen hands, thin, brown, and scruffy, they stuck together like glue as they circled the paddock's edge. Finally, Tom instructed Whip to set the last one free. "But watch out. This one is supposed to be the feistiest. Step back quick after you open the stall."

"Will do," Whip said, jumping up and entering the darkened trailer one more time. As they heard the rasp of the latch pulling back, Whip yelled, "Whoa, boy!"

The door clanged back, and a dun stallion clambered out, rearing up at the base of the ramp. His hooves crashed into the open gate, and the two men holding it in fell back. In an instant, the horse jumped over them and the twisted gate and galloped off across the field. In the paddock, the white stallion went wild, snorting and shrieking as he galloped about and pawed the ground. The other three cowered together on the far side.

"Geez," Tom said. For a second, he thought the stallion might jump the fence or follow the other one, trampling over his men. "Eddie, pull back the truck! Greg and Whip—close the gates now!"

Tom whistled, watching the strong, agile creature put distance between himself and the trailer. Finally, the horse slowed, turning to rear and whinny at his captors. "A Kiger mustang. Now that's something you don't see every day."

Tom untied Blue from where he was hitched to the fence and leapt into the saddle. "Secure the gate. This lot'll be okay for now. I need three of you to saddle up with ropes and follow me ASAP!"

With that, he nudged Blue, and the horse took off. As he neared the dun stallion, Blue slowed, suddenly in no hurry to get closer to the strange horse. The Kiger reared and whinnied again, then began pawing at the ground. Tom wished he'd asked a couple of the crew from Morgan's Run to come this morning. Nick Parker, their resident horse whisperer, would have been invaluable at this moment.

He and Blue began circling the Kiger, trying not to spook him. A few minutes later, Whip and two of the other wranglers approached, each riding a steady stable horse. They all began circling the wild horse, ropes poised and waiting for Tom's word.

"Okay, guys, it's now or never. On my count: five, four, three, two, one." Each cowboy threw his lasso, and three, including Tom's and Whip's, hit their mark around the Kiger's thick neck. The horse was thin but incredibly strong, and he began rearing, bucking, and endeavoring to break free. The three wranglers held on tight, their ropes wrapped around saddle horns as they slowly moved back toward the corral.

"Geez, he's a tough one, boss," Whip said, his arm muscles straining, legs pressed against his horse as he tried to stay in the saddle.

Tom nodded. "Sure is, but he's just scared. Doesn't seem to be aggression. Move slow and keep your horses real steady. I'm gonna put him in the second paddock, let him settle down. I have a feeling that he and the other stallion are going to clash."

Tom instructed his men to open the gate to the other paddock as the others urged the Kiger forward. All at once, with a loud whinny, the horse burst into the corral, his eyes trained on the two mares in the adjacent enclosure. The ropes flew behind him as he galloped to the edge of the fence.

"Lucky he had an incentive," Whip said. "Those mares seem to be his."

"Maybe," Tom said, watching the white stallion at the far end of the corral patrolling the fence and searching for an exit route. "I hope we don't have a major skirmish between those two anytime soon. Get

Purdy and his crew down to fix up a new gate now. Two of you stay and monitor this. I've gotta talk to the boss and make a call."

Tom found Harley at the main stables and apprised him of the situation, securing his okay to call Morgan's Run and ask for Nick Parker.

"They said the Kiger is a real find," Harley said. "Hope we can hold on to him."

Tom nodded. "In more ways than one. I better get back, then."

Harley waved, clearly distracted by the preparations for the time trials. "Good luck!" he called.

CHAPTER 4

Shortly before noon, Leonora Morgan's Volvo pulled up in front of the lower barn. "Hi, guys," she said, waving to Tom and Whip, who were leaning on the fence, observing the wild horses. "I see the new recruits have arrived. Hope they're behaving."

Dressed in jeans, a pale yellow sweater, and boots, the petite wife of their boss looked as lovely as ever, her blonde hair perfectly coifed, green eyes sparkling with warmth. Recovering from her second hip replacement, she limped as she moved to open the back of her SUV.

The men walked down to meet her. "Behavin' pretty good. Mornin', Ms. Morgan."

Leonora waved her hand. "Leonora, please. How long have we known you now, Tom?"

He chuckled. "Not long enough, but I'll try to remember. What can we do for you?"

"It's more about what I can do for you. I've brought lunch, and Ruthie and her friend are right behind me. Little Charlotte wanted to come and see the new ponies."

"That's awfully kind of you."

"Happy to do it! Now, where should I set this basket?"

Tom came forward. "I'll take it. Whip, grab a couple of sawhorses and a board from the barn."

As he stood holding the large heavy basket, an antique green Ford truck rumbled up and parked. A heavily pregnant Ruthie Morgan Langdon slid out of the driver's seat, then turned to unbuckle her two-year-old. To Tom's surprise, Grace McGraw emerged from the passenger side.

"Hey, everybody!" Ruthie called, holding her pudgy child with carrot-red curls. "Okay if we take a peek at the newbies?"

Tom smiled. "Look away, but if they approach, step back from the fence. Hey, Charlotte!"

Children loved Tom, and his boss's child was no exception. She wriggled out of her mother's arms and ran to him, arms up. As he scooped her up, he nodded to Grace as she rounded the truck. "Mornin'."

"Not sure if you know my friend Grace? We went all through school together, including the U of A."

"Sure. Hey, Grace," Tom said. She looked pretty in jeans and a pale mauve sweater, her hair pulled back.

Grace blushed. "Hello. Nice to see you."

"Likewise."

Ruthie looked from one to the other. "Well, that's settled. Let's have a peek at these ponies, sweetie."

Whip set down the sawhorses, a piece of plywood on top, as he and Greg followed Tom to the paddock. They stood a short distance away, watchful as he brought the child near the fence. Ruthie waddled up beside them, with Grace a few steps behind. Grace was afraid of horses and had only ridden a few times in her life. Everything about them terrified her—their size, their smell, their snorting breaths. As the others leaned against the fence rail, she hung back a few feet.

"Pretty scrawny, aren't they?" Ruthie said as Tom lifted Charlotte higher. "Except for the stallion and that dun guy. Nothing a good brushing won't take care of with those two, but you have your work cut out with the other three."

Whip turned away from the corral, eyes on Grace. "You okay, miss?"

Pale and shaking, Grace gave him a wan smile. "I'm kind of afraid of horses."

Tom turned and smiled. "They won't hurt you unless you get in the paddock with them. They're more scared of you than you are of them."

Whip nodded. "They've had a long rough trip. Just lucky we could save 'em from the slaughterhouse."

"Poor things," she said, taking a step closer. Her gaze was riveted on the far paddock as the Kiger paced from one end of the fence to the other. "I've never seen a horse quite like that one."

"He's a Kiger," Tom said, handing Charlotte to her mother. "They're pretty rare, especially down here. More of them up north where I come from, although I've actually never seen one, just heard of 'em."

"Where are you from?" Grace asked.

"Little town in Montana."

"I love Montana," Ruthie said. "What town?"

"Columbia Falls in the Flathead Valley. It's northwest of Missoula."

"Don't know it, but I've been to Missoula. Gorgeous country."

Grace had walked the length of the first paddock, Tom and Ruthie following, and was now standing near the Kiger's enclosure. "He's really special, isn't he?"

Tom grinned. "Sure is, and valuable. If we can rehabilitate him, clean him up and train him, he'll be a great addition. Wild horses are strong no matter what breed, but Kigers are even more so. They're sure-footed and steady. Gentle too, if you can gentle 'em."

As they watched, the dun stallion slowly trotted along the side of the corral, nearing them. Grace's instinct was to jump back, but instead, she stood very still, watching his approach.

Whip came forward to stand on Grace's other side in case the horse reared up. "Look at that. He likes you."

They watched in astonishment as the horse paused in front of the shy, diminutive woman, nickering softly, his nose pressed through the fence.

"Careful now," Tom said as she reached out and petted the round, scruffy nose. "I think Whip's right. He likes you, Grace, but careful. We don't know him yet."

"Yeah, he could be a biter," Whip said, moving closer to pet the Kiger.

As the horse snorted and reared, hooves flailing, Tom grabbed Grace and pulled her back. "Can't say he's too fond of you, Kitteridge."

He held her tightly for a minute, the scent of jasmine and citrus filling his senses. "You okay?" he whispered, setting her down, still holding her hand.

"Fine, just surprised." Her pale cheeks were flushed and she trembled, but she managed a smile as she brushed imaginary dirt from her jeans with her free hand.

"Sure you're okay?" Tom said, loving the feel of her smooth skin. His body temperature shot up twenty degrees.

Grace looked down, suddenly aware of his hand still holding hers. "Yes, fine, thank you." She let go, then, still unsteady, reached out and grasped his forearm to steady herself. "Not as balanced as I thought, I guess."

"Hold on as long as you like," he said, eyes soft as he met hers. *I'd hold on to you forever, babe.*

"Ahem," Ruthie said. "When you two are balanced, we thought we'd join you guys for lunch. As usual, Carmela has made a ton. Then maybe we can help name the new guys, right, Charlotte?"

Tom grinned. "This is so kind of your mom. Guys, why don't you try and rustle up three or four chairs from the barn for the ladies? Wipe 'em off first." He turned to Ruthie. "As for naming, that's the big boss's job."

Hand on one hip, her toddler on the other, Ruthie gave him the eye. "And who do you think is the boss of the big boss? Hmm?"

CHAPTER 5

After lunch, a couple of the guys stayed with the wild horses as the rest of the group headed up to the track to watch the time trials. Ruthie invited people to hop into the back of the truck, and Tom offered Grace a ride, which she accepted.

"This is quite a place," she said, sliding into the front seat of his pickup.

"Never been out before?" Tom asked, gazing over at her before starting the engine.

"Once, with Ruthie, but they'd just finished construction. What a beautiful farmhouse," she said as they passed Tom's home, heading up to higher ground. Acres of fields and tracks lay ahead, as well as the bunkhouses and state-of-the-art stable complex.

He nodded toward the house. "I got pretty lucky."

She looked over, her hazel eyes registering astonishment. "You live there?"

"Sure do. It was built for the previous assistant trainer, Gus Casey and his family, but when they moved east, the bosses offered it to me."

"You *are* lucky," she said. "What a great spot, with the mountains and this lovely valley."

"Yeah, I was bowled over by the orographic effect when I first arrived," he said, "to see how lush and green it is here with all the hundreds of miles of desert beyond the mountains."

She smiled, admiring Tom's rough, weathered features. "It is quite unusual, and a well-kept secret thanks to your boss, Ben Morgan Senior, and a handful of wealthy ranchers."

"Have you lived here your whole life?" he asked as they pulled into the lot behind the stables and bunkhouses.

"All twenty-seven years of them, but living in town is like being in a totally different world. This is where the valley shines, in these gorgeous wide-open spaces."

"Yeah," he said, meeting her eyes. "There's a whole lot of gorgeous around here, that's for sure."

As she felt her face redden again, Grace gave him a shy smile, then turned away to find her friend. *Another minute and I might have swooned!*

"Over here," Ruthie called. "Have you met our Alice?" She referred to a petite woman astride Stella, a tall, beautiful chestnut Arabian. A thick, waist-length braid of blonde hair protruded from the back of the woman's helmet.

"Hello," Grace said. "I'm Grace McGraw."

The jockey nodded, clearly distracted as she glared at another rider on Leo, a gray stallion. "I know you from the hardware store."

"Oh, yes, of course," Grace said, taken aback by the woman's abruptness.

Ruthie led her a short distance away and whispered, "She's pissed that they've hired Rupert, the other jockey. Alice is known on the circuit as a prima donna. In my opinion, they shouldn't have hired her. She's a royal bitch, and I've told my husband that. Not that he listens to me. My dad and Spark love her, and they have the final word. She's an amazing jockey, apparently. It was kind of a coup for them to get her."

"Oh?" Grace said

Ruthie rolled her eyes. "Money. Two billionaires have plenty of it, and I'm guessing they doubled any other offer she got. Come on, let's head down to the bleachers and get a good seat. I'm guessing

Charlotte'll last about fifteen minutes. Thirty tops, if I ply her with treats. Oh boy, here come the big bosses."

Grace turned to spy two tall men, one long and lean with a thick head of silver hair, the other bald and more brawny. She knew the lean one well. Ben Morgan Senior had been coming into the hardware store for as long as she could remember. The other man, his dear friend Spark Foster, she had only seen from a distance when the village was invited out to hear about their plans for building Valley Stables. Her father had wanted to come, so they'd closed the store for a couple of hours and driven out to stand under the tent with their fellow citizens.

"Hey, baby," Ben Morgan called to his daughter and granddaughter. He stooped and held out his arms.

Ruthie allowed Charlotte to slide out of her arms and run to her grandfather. "You just missed Mom."

"We passed her on our way in," her father said, kissing Charlotte and ruffling her curls. "You all get enough to eat?"

"What do you think?" Ruthie said, coming to hug him and his friend. "Hey, Spark, do you know my friend Grace McGraw?"

Spark stepped forward. "I know her beautiful singing voice." He winked at Grace, coming forward. "I went to see my Aria and her sister sing last Christmas, and I distinctly remember you, young lady."

Often mistaken for the actor and politician, Fred Thompson, Spark was a robust, handsome man. Before Grace knew what was happening, he had scooped her up in a bear hug. "Good to see you, darlin'. We just had one of your aunt's incredible lunches. Someday I'm gonna pry the recipe for that burger sauce out of her. My chef Aria has tried to duplicate it, but there's always some key ingredient missing." Spark referred to Gracie Walker, owner and chef at Gracie's Diner, the town's very popular eatery.

Grace laughed. "Good luck with that. The family's tried for years to wrest it out of her."

Spark grinned. "This your first time out to our little farm operation?"

"I've been out for quick visits, first at the village event under the tent when you announced your intentions for the property, then Ruthie drove me out when most of the buildings were up. This isn't like any little farm operation I've ever seen. You've created something truly extraordinary out here, Mr. Foster."

Spark chuckled. "Thanks. My buddy and I like to think big. It's been a lifelong dream of ours." He patted his friend's shoulder. "And it's Spark. No Mr. Fosters around here."

"Hello, Grace," Ben Senior said. "Did my baby give you the grand tour?"

"Yes, including a peek at the wild horses that just arrived."

The Morgan patriarch's blue eyes met her own. "That's where we're headed after the time trials. How did they look?"

"Some seemed a little malnourished, but a couple looked very strong and healthy."

"The Kiger is amazing, Dad," Ruthie said. "Wait'll you see him."

"We've got high hopes for him," Spark said.

"He took a real shine to Grace too," Ruthie said. "It was incredible to watch."

Spark turned to her friend. "Another horse whisperer among us?"

Grace laughed. "Hardly. Truth be told, I'm scared to death of horses."

Ben smiled. "Just gotta get to know 'em."

"Hey, bosses," Tom called as he greeted the men, nodding to Grace as he approached.

"We hear you had a spot of trouble getting the new horses into the corral," Ben said. "Everyone okay?"

"Yup. The Kiger gave us a run for our money, but he's settled in now."

Ben nodded. "Good. We're gonna head down there after this. How are the jockeys doin' with Stella and Leo?"

Tom cleared his throat. "Well, Harley knows better than I do 'cause we've been busy with the mustangs and—"

Ben eyed him, raising his hand. "You know darn well what I'm talkin' about. We're all friends here. Spit it out, son."

"Leo does much better with Rupert. Calmer, less skittish."

"Good to know. That's why we hired him. Has a reputation for working well with nervous horses. We've invested a lot in Leo."

"Yes, sir. Would you excuse me? I'm getting a signal from my boss." Tom waved to Harley, who stood by the fence talking with Rupert. With a quick nod to Grace and Ruthie, he said, "Ladies, always good to see you. Come back anytime," and turned away.

Ruthie grinned. "We certainly will, won't we, Grace? After all, I'm pretty sure they'll want you around to help with the Kiger, right, Tom?"

"Got that right," he said, waving as he headed off.

Spark chuckled. "Always the diplomat, our Tom. Did you see? He didn't want to engage in stables gossip."

Aware she had been staring after the gorgeous wrangler and ignoring her companions, Grace turned back to them. Spark eyed her, a grin on his handsome face. "He's also a great guy."

"Sure is," Ben said, as he looked over at Grace. "And if I'm not mistaken, he has a sweet spot for you."

The feeling's mutual, she thought, sure her face was now as red as a beet. "We're just friends," she said, clearly fooling no one.

Horses and riders began to line up for the first race, saving Grace from further conversation about her relationship with Tom Jacobi. At the end of the second race, Charlotte began to fuss. "Nap time," Ruthie declared. "You ready? If you'd rather hang around I'm sure someone can run you back to town."

Grace stood up. "I'm ready. I promised Dad I'd be back for the afternoon shift." With one more glance at Tom, she walked beside her friend to the truck.

"Dad's right, you know. Tom's a great guy," Ruthie said. "Sounds like he went through hell in the divorce, but he's single now and is clearly interested in you."

"Maybe," Grace replied. *And I'm clearly way too interested in him for my own good!* she thought as they drove away. When they passed by the track, Tom looked up and tipped his hat.

"See what I'm talking about? I rest my case," her friend said as Charlotte began to wail in her car seat.

SUNDAY EVENING CHUCK HARVEY, DIRECTOR OF VALLEY CHORUS WAVED his arms in his usual flamboyant fashion. "That's a wrap, people," he said as the final notes of a song drifted away. The local singing group was practicing for their next round of school visits, which they did every other month at Valley Elementary and Saguaro Middle School as well as the regional high school in Grenville, forty-five minutes from town. This month's selections were familiar and part of their repertoire, so the practice had been short.

As the group dispersed, some hanging around for coffee and desserts, Grace sat with Aria Firorelli and Chuck and his partner, George. Aria was a relative newcomer to the Valley, and Grace's initial encounters with Spark's chef had been somewhat intimidating. Now, after getting to know her through chorus, she found her to be warm and friendly. Aria's new relationship with Jonas Miller, an engineer employed by Foster Enterprises, had softened her. She seemed happier and was no longer spending most of practice flirting with every male chorus member.

Aria gazed at her. "Hey, so Spark told me you were out at the stables. What did you think? Pretty cool, huh?"

"Very."

"That's what billions will get you when you want to start a new hobby," the chef said, smiling. "I mean, I love Spark, and he and his buddy are doing amazing things out there, but they do live in a different world from us ordinary folk."

Gary raised his eyebrows. "This coming from the woman who lives in her own custom-built and professionally designed apartment out at Casa Grande? Talk about another world."

Aria laughed. "You're right. I'm very lucky and very spoiled."

"How's things going with your handsome East Coast engineer?" Chuck asked.

Aria gave him a dreamy look. "Incredible. Now, we've gotta find a man for this exquisite woman," she said, waving at Grace. "Right now, she spends most of her days hiding that gorgeous figure under baggy overalls. She needs a sweetie, and then we'll be all set."

Grace blushed. "I'm fine as I am."

Her friend's eyes glistened with mischief. "There are some pretty hot cowboys out at Valley Stables. We just have to find one who's not brain dead from carousing at the Bulldog or falling on his head too many times."

"Leave my star soprano alone, you big fat bully," Chuck said, winking as he reached over and patted Grace's knee. "The right guy is gonna come along, and he damn well better deserve her, or he'll have me to answer to."

Grace raised her hands in protest. "All right, guys! I don't need a matchmaker or a protector. I'm doing just fine."

As the conversation turned to logistics for the upcoming school concerts, she thought, *Doing just fine? That's a joke. Dad's a mess, I can't even speak to a man without turning bright red, and I haven't had a date in over a year!*

CHAPTER 6

Brother and sister stood in the morning sun, surveying the contents of her U-Haul. Tom had taken Monday off to help Bella move in.

"Let's just throw most of this in the barn," Bella said. "I'll need to move it soon anyway."

He raised an eyebrow, gesturing toward the house. "Have you noticed how much room I have here? Half the upstairs is empty. This is your home if you want it. Why rent something when you can stay here rent-free?"

"Because I'd feel like a moocher. This is your home, and someday, you might fill it with a wife and lots of kids."

Tom laughed. "Yeah, right, and pigs will be flying over any minute. Besides, this is technically not my home. It belongs to Valley Stables."

"You told me they'd sell it to you in a heartbeat for next to nothing if you wanted it."

"That was the arrangement they made with Gus and his family, not me."

"Well, anyway... I want to keep my options open. Eventually, it might be easier to live closer to the clinic or the hospital. Besides," she said, waving at the boxes and furniture, "I really don't want to make decisions about all that until I'm settled in at the job."

"Okay, well, that makes sense. Just point to what you want inside, and I'll take things in while you sort. I can get a couple of the guys to come over and store the rest in the barn."

Tom smiled as they worked side by side. It felt great to have his sister here for companionship, but also because he had worried about her being so far away. Bella was his regret when he left Montana. With their parents gone, they only had each other, and they had always been close.

Tom left Bella to her unpacking and headed over to the barn. The men had just wrestled the last of the wild horses out of the barn and into the paddocks. They'd decided to cede two of the four corrals to the five new horses until they settled in, then slowly begin integrating them into the herd. The other ten mustangs were in the east paddock closer to the race tracks and larger stables on the hill. The newcomers were weeks, maybe months, from saddle training. In fact, it would probably take weeks before they'd even be able to throw a blanket over them. Tom had asked to borrow Nick Parker from Morgan's Run for a few days to assess each one. There was no better gentler of wild horses than Nick.

"Hey, Tom," a voice called, and he turned to spy Harley perched on the fence rail, observing the Kiger. "Quite a horse we've got ourselves in that one."

"Yup. Be interesting to see how he settles in," Tom said, watching the sturdy dun stallion circle the paddock.

"Just got a call from Maggie. They can spare Parker next week, and he volunteered to come up Sunday and take a look at these guys. He'll be working with Patty Monday to assess their health. Three of them aren't looking too good."

Tom nodded. "And they haven't eaten much since they arrived."

His boss hopped off the fence, boots stirring up a dust cloud around him. "So, are the crew in for Friday?"

"Pretty sure there'll be at least eight, maybe ten. Is that okay?"

"Of course. We've got Gracie cooking up platters of sides, Willow's in charge of desserts, and I'll be manning the grill."

Tom grinned at his boss. "Sounds great."

"Ruthie's buddy Grace'll be here, and we hope you'll bring your sister?"

"Thanks, she'd be happy to come." Tom swallowed, his body heat rising at the mention of the woman who had already stolen his heart. "Speaking of Grace, you oughta think about hiring her to work with the Kiger. I've never seen a wild horse take to a person like he did with her. She had him eating out of her hand."

Harley shook his head. "Too dangerous, at least until Nick gives the go-ahead."

"You're the boss."

Harley grinned. "Yeah, right. As if any of one of your wild pack of cowboys listens to me. Okay, I've gotta hightail it. The big bosses are bringing lunch and want to meet. Tell your guys to come grab a sandwich later. There's always a ton."

"Will do," Tom said, then headed into the barn to his small office. He did the paperwork for most of Valley Stables' ordering and operations, forwarding all of it to Spark's fancy accountant in Tucson at the end of each month. He groaned, surveying his desk and its mountain of papers. *Now I know how I'm spending my afternoon*, he thought, clearing a space and shuffling through the pile.

CHAPTER 7

Tuesday, Gracie Walker leaned on the counter, eyeing her namesake. "I heard about the other night in the Bulldog."

Grace shrugged, meeting her aunt's gray eyes. "Got him home."

"Listen to me, pumpkin. He's my brother and I love him, but he's not your responsibility. He and I will have words very soon."

"Leave it alone, Auntie. Talking only makes it worse. He misses Mom, that's all."

Gracie straightened up, frowning as she ran her fingers through her frizzy salt-and-pepper hair, dislodging what looked like a french fry. At over six feet, she towered over her niece. "You have a life, and I intend to see that you enjoy it. My idiot brother has some work to do."

As Grace opened her mouth to protest, the diner door opened and Tom walked in with an attractive stranger with curly shoulder-length brown hair and a lovely, slender figure.

"Hmm..." her aunt whispered. "Looks like our Tom has a girlfriend."

Grace's heart sank. *Shortest romantic fantasy ever!*

"Hey, ladies," he said, arm on his companion's waist as they approached. "This is my sister, Bella. She's just moved to town."

"Well, howdy do!" Gracie said. "First meal's always on the house."

Her niece extended her hand. "So nice to meet you. I'm Grace."

As Bella took her hand in a firm handshake, her caramel-brown eyes sparkled with the same warmth as her brother's. "So pleased to meet you, Grace *and* Gracie."

"She's my aunt."

Bella's freckled nose wrinkled as she looked from one to the other. "So you both work here?"

"No, I work for my dad at Valley Hardware. Are you working in town?"

"Yes, at Valley OB-GYN. I'm a midwife."

After listening quietly, Tom said, "You'd be welcome to join us."

"Yes, we'd love it," his sister echoed.

"Thanks, but I'm picking up lunch for my dad, and he's waiting on me. Enjoy your meal."

"Bye, honey," Gracie said, watching her niece head for the door. "I may stop in tonight."

Grace turned at the door and waved, giving her aunt a rueful smile.

"Sit anywhere, folks," Gracie said. "I've gotta get back to the kitchen. Maria will bring you menus in a sec."

BROTHER AND SISTER SAT IN A BACK BOOTH AND ORDERED BURGERS AND iced teas. When Maria, the waitress, disappeared, Bella leaned over the table and whispered, "So... Grace is interesting, isn't she? Pretty too."

Tom grinned. "Don't start. I'm on the bench and plan to remain there for the foreseeable future."

"Bad idea. Look where you're living," she said, gesturing with open arms. "If anywhere should encourage people to get back up on the horse, it's this place."

"Ha-ha. I could say the same to you. Cowboys way outnumber lovely young ladies around here."

"We'll see," she said, looking down at her hands.

Tom studied her for a minute, then said, "You haven't said much about Flathead. How's everyone?"

"If you're referring to the Wicked Witch of the West, I haven't seen her in months. I heard she and Will moved to Bosman."

Tom gave her a look. "I wasn't asking about Mel and Will." He referred to his ex-wife and his ex-best friend, who were now a couple.

"Yes, you were. She may be your ex-wife, but I know the flame hasn't completely petered out."

Tom nodded as Maria set down their teas. "That's where you'd be wrong. Now, can we talk about something else? Like are you ready to start work tomorrow?"

"Absolutely."

"Why did you hightail it out of Missoula anyway? I'm pretty sure you haven't come clean on that."

Bella's slender fingers wrapped around her tea glass, and she took a sip before meeting her brother's eyes. "It's a long story."

"I'm not going anywhere."

Bella shrugged. "It hasn't been the same since Derrick broke it off. I've been lonely and feeling like I needed a change. Then when things got weird at work, I figured why not move to where my big brother lives."

Tom eyed her. "Weird how?"

"I have...had a creepy colleague, Rachel. She was one of the four midwives in the practice. She's always been friendly, but the past year or so, her friendliness crossed a line into something else. It's almost felt like stalking. She was always leaving little notes and small gifts in my mailbox. Then the touching started. She'd sit by me in meetings and find ways to brush against me, touch my hand or arm, massage my shoulder. I asked her to stop, and she would for a few days, but then she'd start up again. Creeped me out. Her personal hygiene isn't that great either, so her nearness was unpleasant for a lot of reasons.

"Then she started asking to come over to the apartment. I put her off with a million excuses, but it didn't stop. She became more and more insistent."

"Geez, Bella, why didn't you report her?"

"I thought I could handle it. I did finally talk to one of the physicians. She said she'd speak to Rachel. Unfortunately, that made Rachel furious, and she began sabotaging me with the other staff. It was subtle, but really uncomfortable. One of the other midwives came to me and asked what was going on because Rachel had glommed on to her.

"Our working relationship suffered too because she was really nasty and snippy when we worked on patients together. Finally, I'd had it and turned in my notice. The head physician offered to fire her if I would agree to stay, but as I said, I needed a change."

Maria appeared, setting down their plates. "Anything else I can get you folks?"

"We're fine, thanks," Tom said, turning to his sister as Maria moved away. "I'm sorry you had to go through that, sis. I mean, I'm happy to have you here, but that's bullshit. I can hire a lawyer and fight it."

"All's well, my knight in shining armor. The day I left town, they fired her and brought on two new midwives."

"But she's gonna do the same thing to someone else."

"Probably, but not to me. Sometimes you just have to walk away. Not healthy to go back to a place of trauma. Now, let's dig into these amazing burgers, and you can tell me all about this valley you're so in love with. And about the lovely Grace, of course!"

CHAPTER 8

At close to noon Wednesday, the bell above the door rang, and Grace looked up to see Ruthie, dressed in dirt-covered jeans and a canvas jacket. Her friend had clearly come from work, more specifically the acres of gardens in which she toiled daily. "Hey, Grace!" she called, nodding to Wilbur as she passed by the counter. "How you doing, Mr. McGraw?"

He smiled. "Can't complain. You get prettier every day, honey."

"And fat!" Ruthie patted her belly. "I've got about a week left with these jeans, then it's into the really jumbo-sized pants again. Whoopee!" She made her way to the rear of the store, where Grace was stacking bags of seed.

"I need more arugula," she said. "Two of our barrels took in water, and the seeds rotted."

"Bummer," Grace said. "Come on, we've still got some in the back."

The two stood in the long, dry seed room as Grace scanned the shelves. "You've been using Rocket and Red Dragon, right? Which ones are you looking for?"

"Rocket. The Red Dragon didn't get wet."

"Why didn't you send one of the guys to get these?" Grace asked, throwing the twenty-five-pound bags on a cart.

"I'm picking up lunch for everyone," Ruthie said, "and I wanted to invite you to dinner. Harley and I decided to have the crew over. Spur of the moment. We do this on Fridays sometimes. It's a bunch of rowdy guys, Patty, and me, so anytime we can pull in an extra woman or two, we're thrilled."

"Well... I don't know. There's my dad and all. We usually have dinner together most nights."

"Have his sister make him a takeout supper. Please come."

Grace smiled at her friend. "I'd love to."

"Super. Now I've gotta get lunch to our hungry crew."

"I'll throw these in your truck," Grace said, grabbing a sack.

"I'm not an invalid," Ruthie said, taking the other. "You forget I carry around a little thirty-eight pounder day and night."

They said goodbye at the truck. "I'll put the seeds on your account, with a natural disaster discount," Grace said.

"Thanks. See you Friday."

"What time? Can I bring anything?"

"Around six. Don't need to bring a thing. Willow loves to cook, and my husband grills enough meat for an army. Plus, he ordered a bunch of sides from Gracie's. We'll be eating leftovers for a week."

Grace smiled. "Thanks." *I'll have to stop a little early Friday to pick up Dad's dinner and change*, she thought, *as I'm sure "the crew" includes Tom Jacobi.*

CHAPTER 9

"Thanks, Auntie," Grace said as she took the brown bag of takeout. "Dad will love this. I won't be late."

"No worries, baby. I'm going to pop over to the Bulldog around eight and check to make sure he's not there."

"Says he's staying home," she said, knowing that the likelihood of that was slim.

"Uh-huh, we'll see. Don't give him a thought and go enjoy yourself. Goodness knows you deserve it."

Grace stepped behind the counter to give her aunt a wordless hug. No one knew better than Gracie how hellish the past year had been for her niece. Even Ruthie, busy with work and motherhood, hadn't a clue how much she'd endured.

"Enough of that," the gruff restaurant owner said. "Now git!"

JUST BEFORE FIVE, TOM PUSHED THE PAPERS ASIDE, SATISFIED WITH HIS afternoon's work. He stood and stretched, shutting off the lights as his men began bringing the first of the horses inside for the night. His favorite time of day, he walked the circuit from the barn to the stables on the hill, checking on each horse, talking with the men, surveying the condition of the stalls.

The thoroughbreds and stable horses were in for the night when he reached the main stables. He waved to Harley, who was astride his enormous Appaloosa, Pepper. His boss completed almost every day with a ride around the property, and tonight was no exception. "See you in a while!" Harley called, tipping his hat as he and Pepper turned north.

Tom walked the length of the barn, stopping to say hello to each horse, always ending with Blue. The tall gray Trakehner nickered as he approached, bowing his head, inviting the strokes he knew would be coming. "Hey, boy," Tom said, patting the soft nose, horse and man cheek to cheek for several seconds. "Wish I had time for a ride, but I'll come early tomorrow."

He waved to one of the stable hands as he headed out the back door, taking the brook trail back to the lower barn. The western sky was ablaze with color as he headed down to the lower paddocks now bathed in the red and orange lights of sunset. There were two horses still in the near paddock when he reached it, the Kiger and one of the bedraggled mares. Absently, he wondered how long it would be before the mare would allow them to touch her, never mind take a curry brush to her tangled, matted coat. He climbed the fence and strolled diagonally across the open space, the shortest route to the barn. The mare hugged the fence on the opposite side, but the Kiger stood still in the center of the corral, watching him.

Were Tom to take the most direct path, the horse would have to step aside, but the sturdy animal stood his ground, eyes following his every move.

"So that's the way it's gonna be, is it?" Tom said, speaking softly as he neared the creature.

The horse began snorting, hooves pawing the ground. Tom knew he should walk around, giving him a wide berth, but instead, he stepped nearer, reaching out. "Hey, boy," he whispered. "I'm not gonna hurt you."

His hand was inches away from the Kiger's nose when the horse reared. With a loud whinny, he swiveled his massive frame to the side, landed again on all fours and trotted across the paddock to the mare. Tom let out the breath he'd been holding, in awe of the animal's strength and beauty. *If we can gentle you, we've got a real prize*, he thought, watching the horse pace back and forth, his eyes never leaving the man.

~

"Welcome, welcome!" Ruthie called from the kitchen as Harley's daughter Willow opened the front door to Grace.

"Hi, Willow, so good to see you. Are you on college break?" Grace asked, hugging her.

"Hi, Ms. McGraw. No, I'm just home for a couple of days."

The tall, flaxen-haired young woman with haunting green eyes had been conceived during her father's freshman year of college. He and her mother, Talia Goldstein, had split up shortly after, and Harley hadn't learned of her existence until Willow was fourteen and her mother was dying. She now lived with Harley and Ruthie, and sometimes with her grandparents in Flagstaff. Charlotte, her half sister, ran into the front hall, wrapping her arms around Willow's legs. "Come play with me, Willy. Please?"

Willow shrugged, smiling at Grace. "I guess I'm gonna play. You know your way around, right?"

"Absolutely," Grace said, smiling as the sisters disappeared into the family room.

Grace headed for the kitchen, marveling as she always did at the magnificent contemporary home Harley and Ruthie had built. It sat at the northern edge of Morgan's Run Loop Trail on a rise a few miles from Valley Stables. The three-story dwelling had three-hundred-and-sixty-degree views from its windowed walls on all four sides. The open first floor had a massive stone chimney with back-to-back fireplaces in the kitchen and family room. The master bedroom and bath were also on this floor, along with an office area that the couple shared. Three bedrooms and baths were on the second floor.

The third floor was an octagonal living room with a small bar/kitchen, a bath, and a porch that ran all around its perimeter. The porch included a state-of-the-art outdoor kitchen. The octagonal room was furnished with custom-built sectional sofas with several built-in chaises. Since most of the family's entertaining took place on the third floor, they had installed a dumbwaiter to transport food and supplies from the main kitchen to the small bar area in the octagon room.

"Hey, girl," Ruthie said at the long granite island. She was in the midst of patting ground beef into patties, plopping each burger onto an enormous platter. "We're gonna move the party upstairs, but I'm prepping down here.

"Give me a job. I'd love to help."

"How about completing the salad? All the greens are washed, and the other vegetables are there, waiting for chopping," Ruthie said, pointing toward the opposite end of the island.

The women worked side by side, chatting about their day until voices sounded from the front hall.

"The rabble rousers have arrived," Ruthie said, giving Grace a look. "Hopefully my husband will shoo them upstairs."

A short time later, Ruthie's oldest brother, Ben, and his family arrived. The kids, Emma, ten years old, and Benny, or Ben the third, five, raced in to find Willow and Charlotte. Ben headed to the third floor, and Maggie, his wife, popped into the kitchen just as the two women were loading the food into the dumbwaiter.

"Evenin'," she said, flashing one of her radiant smiles. Eight months pregnant, dressed in jeans and a blue, V-necked tunic sweater that revealed just a hint of her glorious cleavage, Maggie looked lovely. Known in the community as the beautiful couple, she and her husband lived up to the nickname. He was drop-dead handsome, and she was one of the most beautiful women in the valley.

"Hey, Mags, you look great as always," her sister-in-law said. Then, eyeing Maggie more closely, Ruthie added, "But on closer inspection, a little tired. Are you okay?"

Maggie laughed, waving her hands, then pointing to her belly. "What can I say? I'm fine, but life is busy and full."

"Tell me about it," Ruthie said, touching her stomach. "Of course, I don't have to run after Ben the wild man."

Maggie smiled, turning to Grace. "So nice to see you."

"You too." Grace came around the island to give her a hug.

A few minutes later, after cleaning up and wiping countertops, Ruthie said, "Well, ladies, shall we go up? We can rescue Willow on our way, poor thing. Not sure which is the most daunting, entertaining the hellions or being besieged by the cowboys upstairs. They're all half in love with her."

Maggie chuckled. "Why wouldn't they be? She's a lovely young woman inside and out."

"That she is," Ruthie said. "And she gets to escape back to her dorm Monday morning."

CHAPTER 10

The party was in full swing when Maggie, Ruthie, and Grace reached the top of the spectacular curving maple staircase that opened into the octagon room. Most of the guests were outside on the wide-open porches. The children had accompanied them up and almost instantly headed back down the porch stairs to the backyard play area, which included swings, climbing apparatus, and riding toys. In her mature, sweet way, Ben and Maggie's Emma smiled at Willow. "No worries, Will, you stay up here and have fun. I'll watch them. Daddy says Jasper's coming, so Ben'll be happy, and I'll play with Charlotte."

Sure enough, as they gazed down at the play area, a little guy with blond curls raced into the yard and grabbed Ben the third. The two instantly ran off together. Ruthie shook her head. "I'm delighted, of course, but I didn't know Harley had asked Kevin and Polly. Hope we have enough burgers."

"Well, at least you've got a few vegetarians who won't need the meat," Maggie said, referring to herself and her husband.

"Meat is no problem, I assure you," Ruthie said. "Harley has a mountain of sausages and steaks he's planning to grill. And we've got enough sides to sink a ship."

"I will gladly forgo meat for all those delicious looking salads and vegetable dishes," Grace said.

"Ignore the burger comment," Ruthie said. "I'm just a grouchy pregnant woman. Hi, Polly, hi, Kevin!" she called as a couple climbed onto the porch, a slender blonde with a dark-haired one-year-old baby on her hip, and her handsome sandy-haired husband. Polly was the head teacher at the Cottage, the day care and nursery on Morgan's Run and Kevin, the contractor whose crews had built all of Valley Stables as well as many Valley homes, including the one in which they stood.

"Hi," Polly said as Kevin waved and joined the men on the porch.

"Oh my goodness, Perry's getting so big," Maggie said, hugging mother and child. "Now that Bennie's in kindergarten in town, I don't get to the Cottage as often."

"She's growing fast, that's for sure," Polly said.

"You know Grace, don't you Poll?" Ruthie asked.

"Of course. Hi, Grace, so nice to see you. We'll be coming in soon for our seeds and pots for our growing unit."

Grace smiled at her. "We'll be ready. Dad and I love it when the kids come to the store." Several times a year, the Cottage children took a field trip to Valley Hardware, sometimes for seeds, other times to see the baby chicks and ducklings that the store carried seasonally.

As more guests wandered in, including another Morgan brother, Robbie, with his wife, Hope Seymour, Grace grabbed a glass of wine and strolled out to the porch to enjoy the view of the valley and mountains.

Peals of laughter came from the play area below as a voice behind her said, "Cute little rug rats."

Startled, Grace turned to find Tom, beer in hand, smiling at her. "I'm not sure their parents would like us referring to them as rug rats."

He laughed. "Where do you think I heard it? Both my boss and his best buddy call their kids rug rats all the time."

"Well, if I ever have kids, I won't," Grace said, smiling at him. In the silence that fell between them, Grace thought, *I could get lost in those dark brown eyes.*

"Penny for your thoughts?"

She hesitated, then took a breath and decided to be honest. "I was thinking about your eyes."

Surprised, Tom gazed at her. "Really?"

"Really," she said, "but don't read too much into it."

"If it's all the same to you, I think I will not only read something into it, but take it as an encouraging sign."

His beautiful smile melted her heart as he leaned closer. She was about to reply when Bella interrupted them. "Help me, big brother. I'm being besieged by cowboys! Oh, hi, Grace. Great to see you again. Is this always the way it is around here?"

Grace laughed. "Not for me, but I don't have your looks or the figure to wear that dress. You look lovely." And Bella did, in a simple beige jersey dress with long sleeves and a V neck, silver necklace and earrings her only jewelry. Above the knee in length, the dress hugged every curve of her athletic body and picked up the light in her caramel eyes. Her strappy matching sandals accentuated her long, toned legs.

"I told you to wear jeans," her brother said. "You're screaming come and get me in that getup."

"Getup?" Bella said, frowning at him. "This is not a getup, and you've always had zero fashion sense."

"I'm just sayin', if you don't want the wolves chasin' you, dress like a cowgirl."

Grace smiled at the brother-sister banter. "I doubt that would help. Bella's the new gal in town, and that pretty much ensures that every cowboy within fifty miles will want to check her out. The fact that she's beautiful and knows how to dress means they'll be in hot pursuit for many moons. You'll have your work cut out tryin' to protect her."

"Ha-ha," he said as Harley joined them. "Hey, Bella, you look hot."

She gave a slight curtsy. "Thank you. Nice party. Thanks for including me."

Then, noticing Grace, Harley said, "Good to see you, Grace. You look amazing too."

An afterthought if I ever heard one, Grace thought. "Thanks."

"I hear you had an interesting encounter with one of our new horses."

Tom nodded. "I told him how you and the Kiger bonded."

Grace blushed. "I wouldn't say we bonded, but he is a beauty, and I loved seeing him up close. I'm usually really nervous around horses."

"I've never seen a Kiger," Bella said.

Harley looked over at her. "I'm surprised with you growing up in Montana. They're a great breed, strong and steady, but gentle if they're domesticated. They make great trail horses 'cause they're sure-footed and don't spook easily."

"I'll take you over and you can meet him tomorrow, sis," Tom said.

"There is gentleness in his eyes," Grace said, surprised at her boldness in speaking up. "There's just something about him."

Harley regarded her for several minutes as the others chatted. Finally, he said, "Excuse me, guys. Gotta get back to the grill before Whip burns all that grade A valley meat. Grace, why don't you and Tom arrange a time for you to come over, maybe after work? I'd like to see you with the Kiger." He turned to Tom. "In fact, if Grace is free Sunday afternoon, Nick Parker from Morgan's Run is stopping by around two. I never say no to volunteers as long as I'm sure they'll be safe." With a wink at Grace, he turned and headed for the grill.

Tom turned to Grace, a wide grin on his face. "Well, there you go. That's a first for the boss in my experience."

"Too bad the boss is married," Bella sighed. "He's the quintessential cowboy, isn't he?"

"His best buddy Ben Morgan's not too shabby either," Grace said. Then, noticing Tom's expression, she added. "You're all handsome cowboys from where I'm standing."

He chuckled. "You're just saying that so my feelings won't be hurt at your swooning over Ben and Harley."

"No, she's not, big brother. You're the most gorgeous man in the place."

"Now I know you're bs-ing me, but if you say you have a crush on Whip, I'll have to fire him tomorrow."

"Dinner!" Ruthie called from the doorway.

"Shall we?" Tom asked, looking from one woman to the other.

Bella grabbed his arm, then Grace's. "Absolutely. I'm starved."

CHAPTER 11

Saturday was always a busy day at the store, and this one was no exception. Grace and her dad scrambled from dawn to dusk to assist their customers as well as make a few deliveries. Their delivery man had recently moved to Prescott, and Wilbur had not yet replaced him despite his daughter's pleas. Grace was strong, but he wasn't, and they needed another worker. During a lull, she brought up the subject again as they worked in the side yard, organizing a delivery of manure, compost, and mulch.

"Dad, we need to hire someone. Two someones, really. This isn't healthy for you, and I'm not able to do what Lurvy used to do. We need strong, able-bodied workers."

"Too expensive," he said, his face red and blotchy from stacking fifty-pound bags of peat moss.

"No, it isn't. Business is good. We can afford it. I do the books, remember?"

"Don't have time to run around trying to find someone."

"I'm happy to do it. Please say yes, and I'll start looking."

"This isn't about extra help, is it?" he asked, eyeing her. "You want to work out at the fancy stables."

"I would be a volunteer, but I can work around my hours here."

Wilbur McGraw stepped back and observed his beautiful

daughter, the apple of her mother's eye. His Essie would never have approved of her working such long hours at the store. Grace had so many talents with so little time to explore them. Guilt washed over him as he thought about what Essie would think of his drinking. "Okay, okay... You win. The Sanchez boy was in a couple of weeks ago lookin' for work. I'll give him a call."

Grace's face brightened. "Paulo? He'd be perfect!"

"We'll see. I'll ask him if he knows anybody else."

"I'll put up a sign at the diner."

"Suit yourself."

"Oh, Papa, thank you!" she said, throwing her arms around him.

He knew very well that most of her excitement was related to working out at the stables with that cowboy Tom Jacobi, but he was pleased he could make her happy. *She's given up so much for me.* "Now, don't get too excited. Haven't hired anyone yet. And we'll have to train 'em."

"We will!" Grace said, heaving the last stack onto the pile.

"We'd better make up a schedule of when you'll be gone so we can know when we need 'em."

"That's easy. We need them full time, no matter what's on my schedule."

"Okay, okay... Now, time for lunch." On Saturdays, father and daughter locked up, hung a "be back at one" sign on the door, and headed over to Gracie's. If his sister was free, she'd join them. If the diner was hopping, they'd sit at the counter and chat as she passed by.

As it was a slow day, Gracie left the kitchen to her assistant cook, Andy, and brought a sandwich to where they waited in a booth at the far end of the restaurant.

"So you're off to see your handsome cowboy today, are you?" her aunt asked, eyeing her niece with a twinkle in her eye.

"He's not my handsome cowboy. Tom is just a friend."

"I have lots of friends, and none of us look at each other the way you two do."

"Ha-ha. Can we change the subject, please?"

Ignoring her, Wilbur said, "Yup, she's got me hiring extra help at the store so's she can spend time with the guy."

"That's not true!" Grace said, frowning at him.

"Well, I support her a hundred percent!" his sister said. "Ever since you lost Lurvy, you've needed someone. In fact, Grace shouldn't be working there at all except in a pinch."

"Not your business, sis."

His sister waved her sandwich at him. "It absolutely is. Essie asked me to look after her, and that's what I'm doing. She needs to spread her wings."

Her brother's face was bright red as he glared across the table. "Now, you look here—"

Grace raised her hands. "Enough, you two! I'm an adult, and I can look after myself, thank you very much."

Her aunt patted her hand. "Of course you can, sweetie."

Grace withdrew her hand and placed it in her lap. "Yes, I'm looking forward to spending time helping out at the stables, I admit. They just got five new mustangs, and there's one I'd like to get to know. However, putting that aside, we need help at the store. Strong, reliable help."

"Which I have agreed to, end of discussion," he said.

Grace picked up her dishes and slid out of the booth. "You two relax and catch up. I'll head back to the store." She leaned over and gave her aunt a kiss on the cheek.

"See you, dearie," Gracie said, smiling up at her.

"Won't be long," her father said.

"THEY'RE BEAUTIFUL." BELLA SIGHED AS SHE AND TOM LEANED ON THE fence, observing the five new horses. "Even the skinny ones. There's a majesty about them, isn't there?"

"Yup."

"Are these all destined for the Border Patrol after they're gentled?"

"Not necessarily. We may keep a few as stable horses. Maybe even sell one or two. Local families are sometimes looking for a family horse."

"Think you'll ever take boarders or offer lessons out here?" she asked.

"So far that's not the plan. Maybe someday. Ben Morgan already has that kind of operation at Morgan's Run. Maggie runs it since Harley came over here."

"I can't wait to see that place too. It sounds very cool."

"There are a lot of cool places around here. You'll see 'em all eventually."

"I'd love to take a trail ride."

"I can take you tomorrow morning, if you like. There are a couple of trail horses up with the thoroughbreds. Long as we're back before Nick Parker and Grace arrive."

"Ah, Grace. It'll be nice for you to have her, won't it?"

Tom gave her a look. "The Kiger took a liking to her. Might be really helpful in helping him settle in."

"Don't be coy, big brother. There's something going on with you two. Don't deny it."

Tom grinned, and the piece of straw he'd been chewing on fluttered to the ground. "She's a nice person."

"She's also not Mel. Time to let go and have a life again. You live in the coolest place in the world. You have an amazing job. What are you waiting for?"

"Enough, nosey. I gotta get to work."

As they strolled back to the barn, Tom smiled. Despite her teasing, it was good to have Bella here. *Too big of a house for one person.*

CHAPTER 12

Nick Parker whistled as he and Tom stepped into the paddock with the new mustangs. "You don't see these guys very often," he said, observing the Kiger paw the dust a short distance away.

"He's a find, that's for sure. Ever worked with a Kiger?" Tom asked.

"Nope, but I hear they're great if you can gentle 'em. Strong and sturdy. They supposedly make superior trail horses."

Tom nodded. "Your boss is already talking about using him for pack trips."

"They sure have the body for it. They all do if you can get them healthy. Ever see the documentary *Unbranded*? It's an incredible film about a pack trip from the border of Mexico to Canada using domesticated wild horses."

Tom nodded. "Incredible story."

"Speaking of that, I hear Ben's been workin' hard to get Harley to go on next month's pack trip. Only seven riders, but he thinks he needs three guides."

"I'm guessing with Ruthie pregnant, he'll never agree."

"What about you, then?" Nick asked, quietly sidestepping toward the Kiger.

Tom shrugged. "We've talked about it, but last I heard, Ben hadn't even booked the trip. I kinda hate to be away with these new guys, and there's a lot going on up the hill."

"You've got Kittredge and Greg. They're pretty reliable. Maggie would kill to have a crew like you guys have out here. With Jeb in school, it's just her, Brendan and me, and a couple of part-timers."

Tom looked toward the drive. "Speaking of part-timers, here comes a potential one right now."

"Isn't that Grace McGraw?"

"Yup."

Nick shook his head. "I didn't know she worked with horses."

Tom grinned. "She doesn't, but the Kiger seemed to take a fancy to her."

"I'd be careful there. Might be dangerous," Nick said as the white stallion in the other paddock reared up behind them with a loud whinny. "Hey, boy," Nick said, raising one arm as the huge horse stomped to the dusty ground and ran off. "He's gonna be a handful."

"She won't be near him," Tom said, waving as Grace appeared at the barn door. "Hey, Grace!" he called, walking to meet her.

Hand over her eyes to block the sun, she approached. As she neared the fence, she called, "Hi, Tom, hi, Nick." She knew Nick from his frequent visits to the store. Much shorter than Tom, he had thick brown hair that stuck out the sides of his hat. Chocolate-brown eyes observed Tom and Grace, just as he'd previously been studying the five horses.

"Hey, thanks for coming," Tom said.

"My pleasure," she said, returning his smile.

Nick sensed movement behind him and turned to see the Kiger watching the others. Suddenly, he whinnied and reared up, galloping straight toward Tom. Instinctively, Tom moved away from Grace, telling her to step back. He then turned to the horse, who slowed down, now ignoring Tom's presence, his huge brown eyes trained on Grace.

"Hey, boy," she said softly.

The horse nickered as he reached the fence, eyes never leaving her as he placed himself between Grace and Tom.

Nick chuckled, remaining in the center of the paddock. "Someone's jealous."

As the two men watched, the Kiger poked his head over the fence, continuing to nicker. With a glance at Tom, Grace came forward. "Hey, good boy," she whispered, reaching out to stroke his nose. The animal responded with more nickering punctuated by sighs.

Mesmerized, Tom's eyes never left the two, especially Grace. "Remarkable," he said, shaking his head.

Nick stayed back, a grin on his face. "Never seen anything like it. If I hadn't just seen him rearing and roaring, I'd swear he's a domestic."

Grace, who had spent her life until now deathly afraid of horses, leaned forward to rest her face against his cheek. "Be careful," Tom said. "I'm pretty sure he's got a healthy set of teeth."

"You won't hurt me, will you, Dusty?" she said, continuing to pat his muzzle and cheek.

Nick tipped his Stetson, smiling. "Dusty? So you've named 'em already?"

"Not yet. The big bosses do that, but Dusty sure fits him."

As the three chatted, Tom and Nick kept a close eye on the Kiger and the movements of the others behind them. The American Paint and the two mares slowly approached.

"Well, would you look at these guys. Curious? Jealous? Whaddya think?" Nick asked, his tone light, even as he kept an eye on the white stallion pacing and snorting in the other enclosure. "He's not happy, is he?"

"The Paint's afraid of him. Not sure about the Kiger. So far, we've kept them apart."

"I'd suggest we work with him first or he's gonna cause trouble," Nick said.

"You're probably right," Tom said, looking over his shoulder as a Mercedes SUV pulled in beside the barn. Tom waved as Spark, Ben Senior, and a petite brunette hopped out. As his bosses and Patty Turner, the resident vet, headed their way, he turned back to his companions, looking over at Nick. "This is where you come in, buddy. I asked Patty to come check them out Monday, but looks like she decided to tag along with the big bosses. Wonder why Harley isn't with 'em." No sooner had Tom spoken than a truck pulled in, and his boss joined the others.

"Hey, guys," Harley said. As he and his employers neared the paddock, the Kiger let out a snort and pawed the ground. "Grace, should you be that close to him? Doesn't look safe."

"Dusty's protecting her," Tom said.

Harley grinned, pushing his hat back and scratching his forehead. "Dusty?"

"Name's subject to approval, but it fits, don't you think?"

"I agree," Ben Senior said. He turned to Spark. "Whaddya think, buddy?"

"Dusty it is," Spark said. As he came closer, Dusty snorted and whinnied, rearing slightly. "Gee, he looked so gentle a minute ago."

"That's Grace," Tom said.

Nick joined the group, one eye on the Kiger. "Yup, you've got a budding horse whisperer here. She sure has a way with ole Dusty."

Never one to be ignored, Patty cleared her throat and stepped up to the fence. "Since Ben and Spark were coming out, I thought I'd ride along and take a look at the mustangs, if you think it's safe?"

Tom shrugged. "Don't think the stallion'll let you get near him, but with Nick's help, you might get close to the two mares and the Paint. I doubt anyone can get near ole Dusty without Grace's help. Why don't you start with the others?"

A frown on her face, Patty nodded to Grace. She walked a few steps, handed her bag to Nick, and climbed over into the paddock. As she and Nick examined each horse, Ben, Spark, and Harley discussed names for the other four horses. By the time Patty turned her attention to Dusty, the others had been named. The Paint they decided to call Rusty, the two mares Star and Swallow, and the white stallion Ghost.

Patty strolled over to where Grace stood, petting Dusty. "He looks pretty healthy, the others not so much," she said, directing her remarks to the men. "The mare with the white patch—"

"Star," Spark said.

She nodded. "Star looks to be severely malnourished. Has she eaten much?"

"Watered-down mash," Tom said. "The other mare too. Paint's eating pretty good, and Ghost has been eating like a...well like a horse. Dusty too."

"I'll pick up some special food tomorrow and will grab some meds for their evening meal and bring 'em back." Ignoring Grace, she stepped closer to Dusty. "Now, let's see about this big guy."

The Kiger snorted and half reared, letting out a whinny, placing himself between the vet and Grace. Wide-eyed, Grace withdrew her hand. "Hey, boy, it's okay."

Tom came to the horse's side, meeting Grace's eyes. "Better take a few steps back, Patty. He thinks you're threatening her."

Patty rolled her eyes. "As if." More snorts and whinnies. "Okay, okay," she said, throwing up her hands. "What do you and the horse whisperer advise?"

As the others watched this little drama, Harley with a shit-eating grin, Nick came to her side, exchanging looks with Tom. Everyone knew Patty had a crush on the assistant manager, and a number of other single men in the Valley. So far, her interest had not been reciprocated.

Nick stood beside the vet. "I'd let Grace calm him down, then you can at least eye him, head to toe. Not sure about his mouth."

"Fine," the vet said. "Let's do it, then."

Patty spent fifteen minutes looking Dusty over. As Grace stroked him, she was able to check his ears and eyes. Finally, she produced a carrot and asked Grace to feed him half so she could peek in his mouth.

After her examination, Patty stepped back, closing her bag. "From what I can see, he's by far the healthiest of the lot. Probably why he's a bit more gentle."

"With some people," Nick said, grinning at Tom.

Scowling, the vet walked a few yards down the fence, hung her bag on a post, then climbed back over. "Yes... Well, I'll bring him a course of meds and vitamins too, just to be sure."

Twenty minutes later, the men left, and Nick went back to the middle of the paddock, circling slowly, observing the mustangs, talking to each in turn. The Kiger stayed by Grace and Tom and even allowed Tom to pat his withers. "He's a mass of muscle, that's for sure."

Grace smiled. "I love him. I can't believe I'm saying this after growing up petrified of horses, but I'd be happy to come back and work with him. We're actually hiring some help at the store so I'll have more free time."

"That'd be great."

"I hate to go, but I promised Dad I'd be back by four."

"No worries," he said, gazing into her lovely eyes. *I could look at you forever, Grace McGraw*, he thought, every part of his body on fire. "Grace, this might be coming out of left field. I hope not. Would you have dinner with me sometime? Maybe a night this week? Whenever you're free?"

Grace looked up from the Kiger. "I'd love to."

He grinned. "Terrific. Is there a good day for you?"

"I'm free most nights. I have Scrabble and chorus, Wednesdays and Thursdays, sometimes Sundays, but I could always skip a night or go after?"

"How about tomorrow night?" he asked.

Grace smiled. "Perfect. Will it be casual so I know what to wear?"

"I was thinking Vermillion?" he said, referring to a farm-to-table restaurant south of town. "It's good and not too fancy."

"I love Vermillion. Always nice to get out of town too."

"Can I pick you up? Seven?"

"I'd love that, thanks."

After an awkward silence, she said, "Well, I'd better get going." She turned and gave Dusty one more petting. "Bye, sweet boy."

After calling goodbye to Nick, she and Tom walked to her car. His arm brushed against hers as he opened the door. "Thanks for coming out today. It was really helpful."

"I enjoyed every minute."

They stood, eyes locked for a few seconds, then she hopped into her SUV. "See you tomorrow, then."

"Yup, looking forward to it."

As she pulled away, she called, "For the record, I didn't feel like your invitation was coming out of left field!"

A huge grin on his face, Tom felt like jumping and yelling like crazy as he headed back to the paddock. *How in the hell did I get this lucky?*

CHAPTER 13

After her second full day of work, Bella was beginning to settle in at Saguaro Obstetrics and Gynecology. She liked the three doctors and her fellow midwives. The staff was friendly and helpful, and she had been given a small office of her own. As she arranged her tiny desk, a tall, slender man popped his head around the corner. Light brown hair fell over his forehead as deep blue eyes met her own. He was dressed in jeans, sneakers, and a wildly colored lab coat that reminded her of Van Gogh's "Starry Night."

Bella smiled. "Hello?"

"Sorry to disturb. I'm Marc Koenig, senior physician. I was on vacation last week, so we haven't met."

"Oh, hi," she said, hopping up. "Great to finally meet you Dr. Koenig. You weren't a part of the zoom interview group, were you?" *I'd certainly have remembered you!*

"No, sorry, it's been a crazy few months. A few of us volunteer for weeks at a time on reservations in the area. I'd tried to patch in the day of your interview, but the Wi-Fi was not cooperating. I did watch the tape, though. We're lucky to have you. Welcome." He continued to lean on the doorframe.

"Thanks, I'm so happy to be here."

"Have you got a minute?" he asked, brushing the errant locks of hair from his forehead.

"Of course, but only one chair. Sorry."

"No problem. Finish what you're doing. My office is 212, just down the hall on the right."

Bella stood. "Just pushing papers around. They said they were working on my schedule, so I'm free now. Does that work?"

"As it happens, your schedule is exactly what I wish to discuss. Follow me."

When they were seated in his office, only slightly larger than her own, he asked, "Want anything? Coffee? Water?"

"I'm fine, thanks."

"Have you sorted out a place to live?"

"For now, I'm staying north of town with my brother. He lives at Valley Stables."

"Well, we can help with finding you something if you want your own place."

Bella shrugged. "I suspect I will, but Tom has a huge house, and I think he's glad of the company."

"Anything else I can help with?"

"Not at the moment. I'm sure I'll have lots of questions as I start seeing more patients. Nancy's been super helpful. I'll make a list as I think of things."

"Right, then." He grabbed a sheet of paper from the side of his desk and handed it to her. "Here's your schedule for today. Nancy's pulling the files and will leave them on your desk, but everything's online as well. Do you have all the passcodes to get into the Valley system?"

Bella nodded as she scanned the sheet, finding only four patients' names. "This is a light day, then? Or is this typical?"

"We try to give patients plenty of time, but yes, this is light. A typical day is usually six to seven patients, depending upon who's assigned to hospital rounds."

"Maggie Morgan?" she asked, reading the third name on the list.

"Yes, aside from welcoming you and answering any questions you might have, she's actually why I wanted to speak with you. Have you met Ms. Morgan?"

"Yes, she's great."

He nodded. "A lovely woman. She's my patient, but insists on being followed and attended by a midwife. The midwife you replaced, Janet Rangely, had been following Ms. Morgan's pregnancy until now. Maggie's eight months along."

Bella nodded, waiting for him to continue.

"I read your file Ms. Jacobi."

"Bella, please."

He met her eyes. "Bella, I read your résumé and paperwork, and I know you've attended many high-risk births. Maggie Morgan had a late-term miscarriage a few years ago, and she's scared to death. I believe you'll be a good match. I will, of course, be there at the birth, or on call, but I think your experience will be invaluable. Our other midwives are terrific, but perhaps not as experienced."

"What happened with her prior pregnancy?"

"She fell from her horse. A very large horse. Took almost a year before she moved beyond the trauma. She's worried this time about miscarrying and afraid that her husband may not want the baby, even though he's being supportive."

"Why would she think that?"

"She's emotional and scared. He is too. He almost lost her last time."

"They seem like a very loving couple."

"They are." He leaned back, running his fingers through his hair. "We'll take the best care of her we can, and him too, if need be. I have recommended no riding."

"Of course. Thank you for your confidence in me, Dr. Koenig."

He smiled, a brilliant, genuine smile. "It's Marc."

As Bella headed back to her office to prepare for her first patient, she mused, *'It's Marc,' indeed. Whether they're doctors, cowboys, or entrepreneurs, this valley is sure full of gorgeous men!*

"HELLO AGAIN, SO NICE TO SEE YOU," BELLA SAID AS SHE STEPPED INTO the examining room with Maggie Morgan.

"Hi, Bella. Marc just told me you'd be my midwife. I'm so pleased. I've been a bit unsettled since Janet left."

"I promise to take good care of you," Bella said, taking a seat beside the examination table.

They spoke for a long while about Maggie's health, her previous pregnancies, and her present fears. Finally, Bella said, "I find it's really helpful to do an exam at this point, then revisit the present-day issues after that. Does that sound okay to you?" She laid her hand on Maggie's. "Please be honest. This is your appointment."

Tears rimming her eyes, Maggie nodded. "That sounds fine."

"Just a quick peek and the sonogram."

As Maggie lay down, she looked over at Bella. "I'm feeling really guilty. Ben should be here. I didn't tell him about this appointment. Even though he's putting on a good show, he's completely freaked out about me, the baby, everything. His hovering is driving me crazy."

Bella smiled as she gently adjusted Maggie's legs. "All that is understandable. Anytime he wants to come, give us a call and you can pop back with him. Ah, here's Leah with the sonogram."

After a gentle examination, Bella took the sonogram wand from her assistant. "Thanks, we're all set. Are you ready to take baby's latest pic?"

Leah nodded and stepped back. A minute later, gel gently applied, Bella moved the wand slowly until the steady rhythmic sound of a heart beating impossibly fast filled the room.

Tears streaming down her beautiful cheeks, Maggie turned to Bella. "It never gets old, does it?"

"It sure doesn't," Bella replied, patting her hand. "Very strong, nice and steady. Still don't want to know the sex?"

"No. The kids have been begging us, but we want to wait till the birth."

"Okay then, everything looks perfect." Bella helped Maggie to sit up. "I'll step out and let you get dressed, and then we can chat."

Thirty minutes later, Maggie rose to leave. They had talked about her family and the miscarriage, her fears and dreams. "Thank you for all your time Bella. I am so grateful to have you as my midwife and I am so glad you've moved to the Valley."

Bella hugged her. "We've got a great team here. You're going to be fine."

Maggie stepped back, wiping a tear from her cheek. "I wish I could believe that. I was in a very dark place for such a long time."

"Miscarriages can be deeply traumatic, but you're strong and healthy and you have an amazing support team."

"Yes, I do."

"And what you experienced was an injury-induced miscarriage. This time, no riding and lots of pampering. I hope you'll bring Ben in next time. I know it's hard to have people hovering over you, but from what you've told me, he suffered with the miscarriage too. He needs to hear the baby's heartbeat as often as possible so you can be happy about this together."

Maggie smiled, her brilliant blue eyes sparkling. "You're right, of course. What days are you here this week?"

"Every day. Wednesday and Friday are prep days this week. Then I'll be full-time with patients from then on. Here's my cell number. If you and Ben want to come, text or call me, and I'll make it happen."

"Thanks, Bella."

"My pleasure." She leaned forward and gave her another hug. Maggie trembled in her arms, but when she stepped back, she was smiling. "Take good care, and I'll see you soon."

CHAPTER 14

"Don't you look as pretty as a picture," Wilbur McGraw said as Grace stepped into the living room. She had dressed carefully for her dinner with Tom in a new viscose knit dress with long sleeves and flared skirt. Soft mauve, its round neck was decorated with three tiny cutouts along the neckline. As she twirled around, Grace felt stylish and daring. In anticipation of the dinner, she had run to Gabriela's, a dress shop in town, and the owner had selected the dress and lovely beige heels that highlighted her slender legs. The price tag had almost prompted Grace to decline and run out of the shop, but then she looked in the mirror and knew she had to buy it.

"Thanks, Papa. How was your dinner?" She had prepared a stew and served it to him before dressing, as her father always ate at five thirty. Though it was too early for her, she often sat with him, then ate later in the evening.

"Fine, baby. A car just pulled into the drive. 'Spect it's your beau."

"He's not my beau. Tom's just a friend."

"Does he know that?" her father asked as the doorbell rang. "When he sees you in that dress, he'll want to be your beau, if he isn't already."

"Papa, be nice!" she said as she grabbed her coat and purse and went to the door.

"I'm always nice."

"All set," she said as she spied Tom on the stoop in a soft brown leather jacket, blue shirt, and black jeans, a striking tie with a silver-and-turquoise clasp round his neck.

Her father called, "Have fun, kids!" as she closed the door behind her.

A bemused expression on his face, Tom had just enough time to shout, "Thanks, Wilbur," as the door shut. "No comin' in to say hey to your dad, I guess?"

Grace shrugged. "Easier this way."

"You look beautiful."

Smiling, Grace thought, *Dress was worth every penny.* "You look pretty amazing yourself. Your bolo is gorgeous and very unusual."

"Cost almost a month's salary a while back, but a group of Navaho women came through our town, and I wanted to support them. Was gonna buy a blanket, but then I spied this."

"They're so skilled, aren't they? I have a bracelet with turquoise that's almost the same color, and I treasure it."

Tom grinned, holding out his arm. "Shall we?"

Vermillion's lights twinkled in the growing darkness as Tom drove in and parked the truck. The drive down had been relatively quiet, each sharing stories about their day. When Tom held out his hand to help her out, his touch sent waves of sensation through her body, awakening feelings that were new and surprising.

"You okay?" he asked, his voice soft. "You're shaking. Are you cold?"

"No. I'm fine, thanks," she said, slipping her hand away.

Tom gazed down at her, his eyes warm as he brushed hair from her forehead. "I'm glad we're doing this. Thanks for saying yes."

"I'm glad too," she replied, knowing she was blushing. Had

another truck not pulled in and interrupted them, Grace felt sure he meant to kiss her. *Am I ready for that?* she mused as they walked side by side to the restaurant's entrance.

Edna Loggins stood at the door, chatting with one of her waitstaff. When she spied them, the round, apple-cheeked restaurant owner smiled. "Welcome to Vermillion, folks. Jimmy'll take you to your table."

The tall, thin twenty-something with bright brown eyes seated them in a window nook at the far end of the room. "One of our best tables," he said, winking as he handed them the menus. "You must know someone. Nancy'll be right over."

When he departed, Grace leaned forward, eyes wide. "Do you know someone?"

Tom laughed. "Do I look like someone who knows someone? This is pure chance, but happy chance."

"Evenin', guys," said a younger blonde version of Edna Loggins as she poured their waters. The tall, maize-colored hammered glasses sparkled in the candlelight. "I'm Nancy. Can I get you something to drink or answer questions about tonight's menu? If you've been here before, you know it changes every night."

Grace looked up at her. "Everything looks incredible. Do you have any recommendations?"

"Everything's great, but they got a flash shipment from the coast today that included the red snapper and sand dabs. Have you ever had sand dabs?"

They both shook their heads.

"Most people haven't, especially around here. They're a small flatfish. They're incredible, and we almost never get them. Fran, our chef... I mean Chef Bissett was over-the-moon excited when he unpacked them."

Tom gazed over at Grace. "Are you thinking seafood?" She nodded. "Shall we order a bottle of white wine to share? Unless you'd like a mixed drink or something else?"

"White wine sounds great. I know nothing about wines, so please order something you like."

"I'm easy. A bottle of Saguaro Winery's Sauvignon Blanc, thanks, Nancy."

"Good choice. Any apps I can put in for you now? Tonight's wontons are to die for. Chef's loaded them with shrimp, and they're really light."

Tom looked over at Grace. "What do you think? Want to share an order?"

"Love to. I'd love to try the fried pickles too."

"You won't be sorry. The pickles are one of our specialties. Be right back with your wine," she said, then disappeared.

Tom grinned. "Fried pickles?"

"One of my mom's favorites. She used to make them all the time."

"Thanks for coming tonight," he said. "You look so beautiful."

Grace blushed as she felt his leg brush against hers under the table. "Thanks, but I think you already complimented me."

"Yeah, but that was before I saw you in the candlelight," he said. *Great as the food is here, I'd like nothing better than to sweep you up and find a dark, quiet spot to make love to you, Grace McGraw.* As he reached across the table taking her hand, Nancy returned.

"Here we go." She uncorked the wine and poured a little into both their glasses.

"Great, thanks," he said as Grace nodded in agreement.

"Pickles and wontons will be out soon. Have you decided on dinner yet or do you need some time?"

"I'd love the crispy corn sand dabs," Grace said.

"Red snapper Vermillion for me," Tom said, handing her the menus.

"Terrific choices. You won't be sorry!" Nancy nodded, then stepped back and headed for the kitchen.

Unaccustomed to drinking, Grace sipped her wine slowly. As they enjoyed the savory, succulent appetizers, they chatted about life. By the time Nancy appeared with their entrees, Grace's wineglass was empty.

"Here we are, folks. Crispy corn sand dabs with cauliflower rice and grilled asparagus for you," she said, smiling at Grace. "And your snapper with corn pudding and sautéed red cabbage sir. Anything else I can get you?" They both demurred. She turned to Grace. "Shall I pour more wine for you?"

"Yes, please, but maybe just half a glass." As Nancy departed with their empty appetizer plates, Grace looked at Tom. "Oh my goodness, this looks delicious!"

Tom nodded. "Sure does, although I'm a little sorry I didn't get sand dabs."

"Well, I'm happy to share," she said, separating some fish and vegetables and sliding them onto the clean butter plate Nancy had left. "Here you go," she said, a wide smile on her face as she handed him the plate.

"Well, now I feel like a whiner. I didn't mean for you to give up your dinner. Let me reciprocate."

"Just a bite," Grace said. "I'm already full from the wontons!"

Tom groaned as he sampled the sand dabs. "Oh my God, I think I'll take an order to go for tomorrow!"

"The snapper is delicious too," she said. They ate in silence for several minutes.

Finally, he said, "So what's an incredible woman like you doing single?"

Grace shrugged. "A combination of bad timing and having my heart broken once or twice. I'm a little gun shy, I guess. There also hasn't been a lot of time between caring for my mom, then working and watching out for Dad. He used to have guys working at the store, two or three during our busiest seasons, but as they went on to other things, he didn't replace them. It's been really hard the last couple of years. Scrabble nights and chorus are the only activities that are mine."

"And this," Tom said as he lifted his wine in toast.

She nodded. "Yes, and this is lovely."

"I'm sorry you had your heart broken. Heartbreak sucks, if you'll excuse my language."

She watched him move food around on his plate, refusing to meet her eyes. "Sounds like you're speaking from experience?"

He nodded, looking up. "I went through a pretty messy divorce five years ago. My wife ran off with my best friend."

"How awful." She set down her fork and reached for his hand. "I'm so sorry, Tom."

"I'm doin' okay now, but it's taken me almost five years to find my balance. They were my best friends. Losing them both in one fell swoop was tough. Coming to the Valley has helped put some distance between me and old ghosts."

Grace smiled. "Let's make a pact. Letting go is a priority. The present holds so much promise. We should focus on it."

He smiled, a soft warm smile. "I like that 'we.'"

"I mean... What I meant is—"

He reached over and squeezed her hand. "I know what you meant, but a guy can hope, can't he? Fact is, I'd like nothing more than to kiss you right now."

Her body on fire from head to toe, Grace slipped her hand back across the table. "Might be a little awkward, don't you think?"

"The night is young," he said, enjoying the last bite of his dinner.

Nancy appeared shortly after and asked about dessert. At her suggestion, they decided to split a meringue cream torte that Nancy declared to be "light as a feather and oh so good!"

She was right. As the last crumbs of the torte disappeared, Grace said, "Note to self. If I ever come to Vermillion again, Nancy will have to be my personal orderer."

He laughed. "I'm guessing everything on the menu would have been fantastic, but you're right, Nancy steered us right. Want coffee or anything?"

"No, thanks, I'm perfect."

CHAPTER 15

After Tom paid the check, they strolled out into the cool evening. A pebbled walkway circled the property. Walking it was a favorite after-dinner activity of Vermillion diners. Tonight, the path shimmered with twinkle lights.

Tom looked down at her. "It's a bit chilly, but I've heard that it's a very romantic stroll."

"It's a bit cool out," she said as a shiver passed through her.

"You cold? Want my jacket?"

She gazed up at him, her eyes dreamy. "Your arm around my shoulders should do the trick."

Tom smiled, drawing her close. "You never cease to amaze me."

She leaned against him, drawing warmth from his strong chest and arm. *I could stay like this forever*, she mused, letting out a sigh.

They walked the circle, then headed for the truck. Tom opened her door, then turned and took her into his arms. "Would it be okay if I...?"

"Kissed me? Yes, it would," she whispered, standing on tiptoes as he bent, lips finding her own. Grace opened herself to him, sinking into the sensations of their deep kiss as his hands moved up and down her back, then her sides, flirting with round edges of her breasts.

Suddenly, he broke the kiss and pulled back slightly. "I would love to take this further. You don't know how much I'd love to take this further, but this might not be the best place, baby."

Weak kneed and limp, Grace nodded, then turned to pull herself up into the truck. Suffused with warmth and sensations that startled her, she thought, *What's happening to me?*

Tom closed the door and walked around to his side. Once inside, he turned to her. "Sorry, if I got a little carried away."

"We got carried away. And there's no need to apologize. I loved every second."

"It's times like this that I wish I had my old Ford Fairlane. It had a huge backseat. Not that I used it for...you know."

Grace smiled. "Handsome guy like you? Yes, I know."

They rode back in silence, Grace thinking about old model trucks with full front seats. Not being able to touch him was almost painful. When he pulled up in front of her house, the living room lights and a porch light were on, but the rest of the house appeared to be in darkness.

"I hope that means he's gone to bed," she said, opening her door and hopping out.

Tom came around, took her hand and they strolled up the walk together. "I can come in and help carry him upstairs if you like?"

Grace let go of his hand and climbed the porch, peeking in the window. "Looks like he's gone up. Empty glass means he's probably home and didn't sneak over to the Bulldog."

Arms around her waist, Tom drew her close. "Awful burden for you. Has he tried to get help?"

"He spoke to our pastor, and my aunt Gracie helps when she can. It's not all the time. Only goes on a bender a few times a week. The night you helped me was my mom's birthday."

Tom stroked her forehead, gently brushing strands of hair back as he bent and kissed her brow. "My sweet, beautiful Grace. Please tell me how I can help you."

"This is perfect," she whispered, arms circling his shoulders.

Their lips found each other, tongues expressing a longing and primal passion.

As he trailed kisses down her slender neck, he said, "You've woken something in me that I never knew existed."

"Me too," she said, fingers running through his thick, soft hair. "Unfortunately, this porch is no better than the Vermillion parking lot."

"We'll do better next time. And I hope next time is soon."

"I'd love that."

"How 'bout this Friday? I'll think of some place special."

As they embraced, Grace felt his erection brush against her belly. "Any place is fine."

Tom chuckled. "I'll give it some serious thought. Will we see you out at the stables any time soon?"

"Dad says he's hired Paulo... Paulo Sanchez. He's scheduled to start working tomorrow. If he settles in, I was thinking of taking a half day Wednesday and heading out to see Dusty after lunch."

"That'd be great, but why don't you come have lunch with me? I'm sure I can whip something up."

"I'd love that. Is one too late?"

"Perfect, but I'm not sure how I'll make it till then," he said, drawing her close for one more kiss.

As she watched him walk to the truck, Grace's heart was pounding so hard, she feared it would fly out of her chest. *How many hours till Wednesday afternoon*, she mused as he waved and drove off.

CHAPTER 16

Paulo Sanchez and his friend, Joe Davis started work Tuesday morning. Both men were broad shouldered, strong, and hard workers. By prior arrangement, Grace and her father had decided that he should train them and Grace would work mostly on paperwork long neglected. From time to time, she overheard snippets of their conversation, but for the most part, she closeted herself in the office. Shortly before noon, she emerged and asked the men if she could grab lunch for them. "After all, we want to celebrate your first day with us," she said as the four stood together in the front section of the store.

Paulo grinned. "Thanks, that'd be great."

After taking the orders, she grabbed her purse. Her father gave her an odd look as she passed by on her way out, but she wasn't sure how to read it.

At the end of the day, after the two men had left, father and daughter were closing up the store. "So, how'd it go?" she asked. "Do you think they'll work out?"

Wilbur hmphed. "Paulo's a good worker. Known him all his life. Great kid. Don't trust the other one. He's new in town. Hangs with a bunch of punks."

She smiled at him. "Punks? Didn't know there were any punks in Saguaro."

"You know who I mean. The lazy good-for nothings that can't keep jobs more than five minutes. They usually hang around the market lot till Ty and his men roust 'em out." He referred to Ty Boone, the local sheriff.

"Your call, Papa. You're the one who'll be working with him. If you don't like him, we'll keep looking."

"I'm gonna give him a few days. See how he settles in, then I'll decide."

"Sounds like a good plan. I'm going to head home and start dinner."

Instead of going directly home, she decided to take a stroll down Main Street for some fresh air. As she started out, her cell phone pinged. It was Tom.

Smiling, she answered. "Hello."

"Hey, am I interrupting?" he asked.

"Not at all. I'm just talking a walk after work to clear my head. The store can get pretty musty, dusty, and close." She headed for the deserted park just down the street and sat on a bench.

"How was your day?"

"Same ole same ole. My dad hired two new guys. One's great, the other he's not sure about."

"Hiring's a process."

They talked for a while about the stables and horses. Of course, Grace wanted to hear how Nick had done with Dusty.

"Ghost is giving us the most problems," Tom said. "Dusty's still standoffish except with you. He misses his muse."

Grace leaned back, smiling. "Muse, huh? I like that." As she spoke, she sensed someone approaching from behind. When she turned, she saw Joe. He winked at her, then strolled across the park to sit on a bench, pulling out a cigarette. She couldn't say why, but that wink sent a chill up her spine. Joe had been friendly at work, but a few times she'd found him staring at her. His ogling unnerved her.

"You're certainly my muse," Tom said. When she didn't immediately reply, he asked, "Grace, you okay?"

"Hold on a sec, would you?" she asked, standing. With a quick nod to Joe, she walked back onto the sidewalk and headed for the house a short distance away. When she reached the porch, she was out of breath. Her breathlessness wasn't from exertion, but from an anxiety she couldn't explain. "I'm home," she said, sitting on the porch step.

"Everything okay?"

"Yes, I was sitting in the park, and I got a weird feeling about one of our new workers. He suddenly appeared like he'd been waiting for me or following me. I'm sure it was just a coincidence that he showed up. I guess my dad's comments about him made me paranoid."

"Where's your dad?"

"I imagine he's in the kitchen." She stood and peeked in the front windows. Wilbur was, indeed, puttering around in the kitchen.

"What's going on, Grace?"

"I'm so sorry. Overactive imagination, I guess. All's well. I'll explain when I see you. Forgot to ask before, was there a reason you were calling?"

"Just wanted to hear your voice and couldn't wait till tomorrow."

She smiled, her breathing returning to normal, comforted by his deep, strong voice. "I'm glad you called. Sorry to worry you."

"I think you know... I mean, we've only known each other a short time, but you are precious to me, Grace."

"And you to me," she said softly.

"So, are you inside now?"

She rose and opened the front door, stepping inside and locking it. "Yes, safe inside. Wild imagination tamed, time to start dinner."

"Okay, I'll let you go. See you around one tomorrow, right?"

"Right. Good night."

"Night."

Grace clicked off, holding the phone to her chest, wishing his arms were around her, protective and strong.

Her father's voice sounded from the kitchen, snapping her out of her reverie. "Hey, darlin'! You gonna start dinner anytime soon? This man is starving!"

"Coming Papa! Food just needs warming up." She removed her work boots and slipped into her comfy slippers that sat by the door. *Safe.*

CHAPTER 17

The next day, Grace decided to attribute her anxiety about Joe to an overactive imagination. She said nothing to her father and managed to avoid their new employee for most of the morning. At noon, Paulo and Joe returned from deliveries just as she was saying goodbye to her dad.

"Hey, Grace," Paulo said.

"Hi, guys," she replied, grabbing her backpack from behind the counter.

"Going somewhere?" Joe asked, pointing to the pack.

"Yes. and I'm a bit late. See you. Papa!" she called as she headed for the back door. At home, she changed into clean jeans and a sweatshirt, then jumped in the car and drove north out of town toward Valley Stables. Tom had said to come to the house and they could eat on the porch or back terrace before heading down to the paddock. He was sitting in a rocker waiting when she pulled in, a mile-wide grin on his handsome face.

He walked down to greet her. "Hey, you made it. Right on time." As Grace shut the car door, he swept her up in a warm embrace.

"Hi, so glad to be here." She held on, wishing she could stay in his arms forever.

"Little cool today, so I've set everything up inside. Bella's at work, so it's just us. Come on in. I'll give you the five-cent tour."

In the style of many western homes, a wide porch circled the entire house, affording magnificent views of the valley and mountains to the east and west. The farmhouse had a center chimney. As they stepped inside, Tom gestured around the living room, sparsely furnished with boxes piled along one wall. "Work in progress. Waiting for me to buy some furniture and build bookshelves."

He led the way down a short hall to the master bedroom. "This room, I did furnish."

"Oh it's lovely," Grace said, gazing around at the rough-hewn, king-size four-poster bed with matching dressers and side tables. A colorful patchwork quilt covered the bed, its hues echoing the blues, greens, and reds of the rugs scattered over the room's wide pine floors. She glimpsed a spacious bathroom with an enormous shower and a claw-footed tub. "Wow!" she said, peeking into the room where colorful Mexican tiles brightened the space.

"Yeah, it's pretty cool. Bathrooms were all designed for Gus and his family under Spark's supervision. Spark never does anything halfway."

"It's beautiful," she said, following him down another hallway past a pantry and into the home's beautiful designer kitchen. A granite island dominated the room furnished with burnished cherry cabinets. The sunny, west-facing breakfast nook was lined with window seats. The kitchen opened into a comfortable fireplaced family room with leather sofas and chairs and wide pine floors covered with vibrant Navaho rugs.

"The rugs are amazing," Grace said.

"My passion...or one of my passions, collecting Navaho rugs and blankets. Come on up," he said, leading the way to the stairs.

Upstairs were two bedrooms and two baths with a small extra room at the west end. "Could be an office," he said. "If Bella stays, could also be a small studio office for her. I have my little study off the master, so I have no need for it. It's kinda small, but I think the Caseys planned to make it into a bedroom for their third child. Babies don't need a lot of space, right?"

Grace gave him a look. "Babies have a lot of equipment."

"That's what my sister tells me. Her practice sends home a crazy long list of all the 'essentials' for new babies. So, you ready for lunch?"

"I am."

"Nothing fancy." Tom took her hand as they walked back downstairs to the kitchen. "I've got BLTs. Do you like them?"

"Love 'em."

"Great. The ingredients are all set. We can build our own, or you can relax and I'll make one for you?"

"I'll relax later. Let me make mine," she said, smiling.

They toasted bread, assembled sandwiches, then took them to the breakfast nook, sitting side by side on one of the window seats. He poured them each an iced tea from a pitcher on the table and raised his glass in toast. "Enjoy."

They ate in silence for several minutes, then Tom asked about Joe and her strange encounter the night before. Grace recounted the events and her dad's words.

"I avoided him this morning and will ask Dad what he thinks tonight. It's strange. As I was heading out to come here, Joe asked if I was going somewhere. There was something about the way he asked. I mean... Under a circumstance like that, I'd usually say yes and tell the person where I was going, but I said nothing, just hurried out. His query somehow felt intrusive, but I'm not sure why."

"Trust your gut is my advice. Our guts are usually accurate. And don't be alone with the guy."

Grace shrugged. "I'll see what Dad says."

Sandwiches long gone, they sat chatting and sipping their teas. As they talked, Tom stroked first her hand, then her thigh. Grace found his touch both comforting and sensual. "What a lovely home you have here." She sighed dreamily as her arousal grew.

"I'm lucky." He turned, his eyes meeting hers, his desire mirroring her own.

Before Grace knew what was happening, they were kissing, hungry for each other. Tom pulled her closer, his hands moving down to cup her breasts, and she sighed, giving herself to his touch.

"I've been waiting to do this for thirty-eight painful hours. Is it okay?"

"Yes," she whispered, drawing closer, her body pressed against him, her hand moving down to his cock that now strained the fabric of his jeans.

Tom pushed back from the table and lifted her in his arms, then carried her back to the bedroom, his lips everywhere. When he reached the bed, he laid her down gently, his eyes warm as he gazed down. "You're the boss here. We can stop at kissing, or a little light fooling around? Or...?"

Grace smiled, looking up, loving the curve of his jaw, his soft brown eyes and the way his thick curly hair fell over them. "I'm not that experienced in all this, but I'd say we're way past the light-fooling-around stage, wouldn't you?"

"Well, yeah, but I don't want to force anything on you."

"Do I look like I'm being forced?" she asked, sitting up and pulling her T-shirt over her head and tossing it aside to reveal her round perfect breasts in a delicate lacy white bra. "Maybe you can help with my jeans?"

"Like I said the other night, you are full of surprises, Grace McGraw." Tom unbuttoned then slipped her jeans off, throwing them on a chair.

She laughed, arms open as she reached up to him. "I've been surprising myself too."

"You are the most beautiful woman I've ever seen. Do you know that?" He knelt beside the bed, lips trailing kisses from her neck to her breasts, his tongue licking as he traced a line to the edge of her bra, parting the lace with gentle fingers, then slipping the bra over her head so he could take one breast, then the other into his mouth, sucking and teasing her nipples to ripe, hard buds.

Grace cried out, arching up. "Oh, oh, oh! Please, Tom!"

He stood up, removing his shirt and jeans, reaching into the drawer of his bedside table to grab a condom. "Will we need this, do you think?" he asked, coming to lie beside her, his cock straining for release from his boxer shorts.

Grace massaged his strong, muscular chest, marveling at the man who lay beside her. "Oh, I hope so," she replied, sliding closer until their bodies touched in all the right places.

Tom's hands moved down her smooth, slender hips, caressing as he removed her panties, then his boxers. Their hands were everywhere, until his fingers began a slow, languid walk down her belly, parting her legs and moving up to her warm wetness. Her clit pulsated under his touch as his fingers then lips sent her to a rip-roaring, explosive climax.

So strong were the sensations flooding her body, Grace wondered if she'd been possessed. "Tom, Tom," she moaned, stroking him, begging him. "Please, Tom."

He nodded, slipping the condom on, pulling her closer as he plunged into her warm depths. With slow movements at first, their lovemaking intensified as Grace matched his every thrust, pleading with him to go "deeper and deeper."

"Whatever you say," he said, voice husky as he grasped her ass and pulled her closer.

They locked eyes, their passion mirroring each other's as they reached a crescendo, their simultaneous orgasms rippling through their bodies, no longer two, but one.

After as they lay side by side, Tom's lips found hers for a soft kiss. He then kissed her nose, forehead, and neck. "That was amazing. You've given me such a precious gift."

"You too, me," she said, kissing his chest.

They drifted off to sleep for a short time until he noticed the clock on the bedside table. "Geez." He rose on one elbow, kissing her awake. "Hey, baby, while I'd like nothing better than to stay in this bed for the rest of my life, I promised Nick we'd be down around two."

"Of course." She kissed him back. "What next?"

Tom groaned as he moved away and stood. He shrugged into his shirt and jeans, setting her clothes beside her. "Sorry to cut this short."

"Don't be. Now I can watch you get dressed. You're quite a sight, you know. Do you see my bra anywhere?"

Ten minutes later, fully clothed and put together, they walked arm in arm to the kitchen. Tom grabbed two waters from the fridge and said, "Ready?"

"No, but duty calls," Grace answered, smiling. "It'll be fun to see Dusty."

"One more for the road," he said, pulling her into his arms for a searing, knee-knocking kiss with lots of tongue and wandering hands.

"Now, how am I going to walk?" Grace smiled, her legs like limp noodles as they headed out the back door.

He curled his arm around her waist as they stepped into the sun. "Don't worry, baby. I've got you."

CHAPTER 18

Tom was needed up at the thoroughbred stables, so Grace spent the remainder of the afternoon with Nick and Dusty. After three days of working with him in the round yard, Nick had gotten Dusty comfortable with a soft rope harness and lunge line. The experienced trainer made the harnesses himself because he claimed they were gentler, especially for the wild horses. His only other tool was a stick trainer, also of his own devising. In a short time, Dusty had learned some simple commands, including the clucking sound Nick used for "go." By day three, Dusty was already allowing Nick to pick up the rope as he circled the fence, changing directions at the trainer's signals.

Grace watched from the fence, and Nick narrated what he was doing. "You sometimes see people using these sticks with a whip or rope on the end, but I find this works just fine and is less frightening. I use it for one purpose—as an extension of my hand and arm—never to correct or punish." As he spoke, his eyes never left Dusty.

The two mares and Rusty were in the adjacent paddock, and they occasionally came to the fence to watch trainer and horse. Dusty usually paid them no mind or paused briefly, giving them a friendly nicker before moving on. His primary focus when not following Nick was Grace, and he almost always paused for a pat or nuzzle from her as he circled the paddock.

After an hour, Nick said, "Let's give him a five-minute break, then you can try if you're ready." He climbed up to sit on the fence near where she stood. Dusty followed and nuzzled her shoulder through the fence.

She petted him, then turned to Nick, eyes wide as saucers. "You mean go in there?"

Nick grinned. "Only if you want to. Horses sense fear, so we don't want that. I could be with you, but that might be confusing for Dusty."

"Do you think I'm ready?"

"Wouldn't have suggested it if I didn't think so, but it's your call. For what it's worth, I've never seen a wild horse take to a person like this one does to you. Getting a wild horse to look at you sometimes takes weeks or months. I can't say he'll be a little angel every minute, but I trust him. He's a gentle, steady guy, and he clearly loves you."

Grace listened to the strong, handsome cowboy, his brown eyes kind and calm. The man exuded a peacefulness that was contagious. Horses sensed this and responded, as did the people around them. "Okay, I'll try."

"I haven't been using the stick, and you probably won't need to either, but to be safe, drop it on the ground near you. Ready?"

Grace nodded, then went to the gate and let herself into the paddock. Dusty followed, but Nick kept himself between them until she locked the gate. He then handed her the thin, flexible training stick. "Ready to take the rope? Then you just head into the center and give him a cluck like I've been doing. He might be a little confused at first, but he's smart. He'll catch on."

Grace took a deep breath and walked to the center of the ring. *You can do this, you can do this*, she thought, gaze on Dusty.

"Remember to relax," Nick called. "You relax, and he will too."

Dusty trotted around the paddock for a few minutes, then stopped and looked at her. Softly nickering, he approached and bowed his head, clearly wanting to be petted.

"Hey, boy," she said, patting his muzzle and forehead. Dusty sighed and rubbed against her. "Good boy, good boy," she whispered, then looked over at Nick. "Is this okay? Should I be doing something?"

"You're doing great. Most times, I wouldn't suggest this, but since he's crazy about you, you can try walking beside him with the lunge line. Only if you're comfortable, though. Don't want to rush things."

Grace took the lunge line and clucked, moving toward the fence. When they reached the perimeter, she began walking along the fence line, Dusty on the outer edge beside her. A few minutes later, she began to let out the rope, the lunge line slack as she stepped back to the center of the yard. Still hugging the fence, Dusty paused and looked at her.

"Give him a few clucks and guide him with the line," Nick said. "He'll get the idea."

Sure enough, Dusty responded immediately and began trotting along the fence.

When Tom returned an hour later, he said, "Will you look at that." He stood beside Nick, unable to take his eyes off the beautiful woman he'd been making love to only hours earlier. *Making love? This is love*, he thought. Finally, he turned to his companion. "Is that safe?"

"Ordinarily, I'd say no way, but he's pretty gentle. Haven't seen any aggression except when he spies Ghost. He's crazy about Grace. She's got him eating out of her hand. If you want, I can work with one of the others, maybe Rusty, for the next few days if she's here. See how that goes? I can also try to work in the other round paddock with Ghost if it's free."

"Not unless someone's watching her. I may be able to sparc one of the guys to be here. I know the two of them look nice and cozy, but I don't want Grace alone with him. Not yet."

Nick nodded and was about to speak when Dusty spied Tom and whinnied, stamping his hooves, pulling away from Grace and charging the fence. "Maybe not you, though," the trainer said. "He's very protective of her."

"Well, so am I," Tom said, reaching out toward the approaching horse. "Hey, boy."

Dusty bobbed his head up and down.

"And that doesn't mean yes, I like you," Nick said. "Tom, why don't you give him a wide berth, and Grace, come stand here beside me and see if he'll still come to you."

She came to stand next to Nick, who was now a few yards away from Tom. Dusty settled, turning away from his rival and trotting to her. "Good boy, good boy," she said, patting him.

"Hey, guys," Nick said. "I've got evening chores back at Morgan's Run. You got this?"

"We can leave him out for now," Tom said, heading for the gate. "Grace, can you unclip the line? The guys'll be coming to take them in for dinner soon."

"I've got to run too," Grace said, nuzzling Dusty one more time before climbing the fence. "Bye, good boy," she said as the Kiger paced back and forth in obvious distress.

"We'll work on 'bye-bye' next time," Nick said. "He's gotta get used to your comings and goings. Even though it's cute, that's not acceptable behavior for a gentled, stable horse. We can also try light grooming. I'm pretty sure he'd let Grace run a curry brush over him."

"Not without you holding him," Tom said as the three strolled toward the barn.

"Night folks," Nick said as he headed for his truck. "You comin' tomorrow, Grace?"

"In the afternoon, if possible. Thanks, Nick. This was unbelievable."

"Sure was," he said, tipping his hat.

CHAPTER 19

The lovers stood side by side, watching Nick drive away. As the dust settled on the drive, Tom took her hand. "How are you doing?"

"Great. Thank you so much for this opportunity."

"My pleasure, but I don't want to take chances, Grace. You're precious to me, and that's a wild horse back there."

"I trust him."

"It's still very new. Promise me you'll take things slow."

"Oh, you mean like us?" she asked, smiling mischievously as she gazed up at him.

"Do you really have to go?" The longing in his eyes made it clear that he had other ideas.

"Yes, I do," she said, hands on his chest, loving the feel of him.

"Okay, but before you go, I have something to show you." Tom took her hand and led her into the deserted barn. As soon as they stepped inside, he whisked her into the first immaculately clean stall with its mounds of fresh hay.

"This is nice. Who lives in here?" she asked, knowing full well why he'd dragged her in there.

"You and me, baby," he said, lifting her up and wrapping her legs around his waist as his lips captured hers in a searing kiss. He leaned back, careful of her legs as his shoulders rested against the rough stall wall.

"I think the stall's occupant might beg to differ?" Grace said, as she draped her arms around his shoulders.

"I want you so bad, Grace. I haven't been able to think of anything else since I left you with Nick. I made so many mistakes up there because I literally couldn't get you out of my mind. Then when I came back and saw you with Dusty... I couldn't breathe."

"Well, that's not good." Playfully she kissed his neck. "What's the solution, do you think?" As she spoke, she unbuttoned her jeans. "Care to help a lady in this awkward position, cowboy?"

After looking over his shoulder to make sure they were alone, Tom set her down and helped her out of her jeans and panties. She stroked him through his jeans, then undid the button and released him. "Are you sure, baby?" he asked.

Grace nodded, arms circling his shoulders again. "Take me to the moon. I'm ready for the ride of my life."

Slipping a condom from his pocket, Tom slid it on, then leaned back, lifting her again and wrapping her legs around him, his hands on her ass as he entered her. He intended to go slowly, but Grace was already on her way, urging him on, her body begging him in every move to go deeper and deeper. As their lovemaking reached its peak, she cried out in a glorious orgasm. "Geez, baby," he moaned as she collapsed against him.

It was at that moment they heard voices. The wranglers coming down to take in the horses. "Hey, anyone here?" a voice called. Whip.

Tom grabbed her, reaching over to slam the stall door shut. "Go around the barn, okay, fellas?" he called. "Be out in a sec."

"Sure thing, boss!" Whip called, followed by a chorus of snickers.

Grace looked at him wide-eyed. Her bright red cheeks matched the glow of her rosy, sex-sated body. "Oh my goodness! How embarrassing! We'll never live this down."

"Oh, yes we will. When I get through with them, they won't dare say a word." *Yeah, right,* Tom thought as they both burst into laughter. *I may be their boss, but this story'll drive me nuts for many moons.*

Fully dressed, they strolled to Grace's car hand in hand, then shared a more chaste, gentle hug and kiss before saying goodbye.

"Will I see you tonight at Scrabble?" Tom asked as he closed the truck door behind her. "I just joined 'cause Bella loves the game."

"Absolutely," she said. "Unless Dad needs me. I may be a few minutes late."

As she drove away, Tom's chest constricted, the loss of her warmth excruciating. *No doubt about it, buddy. You're crazy in love with this woman, and there's not a goddamn thing you can do about it. Now, to deal with the yahoos out back*, he thought, rounding the barn.

~

"So I guess you had a fun day, big brother," Bella said as she assembled ingredients to make shrimp tacos. "And to think I missed all the fun."

"What were you doing back there?" He gestured to the hall leading to his bedroom.

"Had to do a load of laundry and the door was ajar. Couldn't help but notice the mussed bed. Since I know what a neatnik you are, I doubted it was in that state when you left this morning. And...you didn't exactly clean up the kitchen after your lunch for two!"

"All right, Sherlock, give us a break, will you?"

"Not quite finished. I know the what and where, but wondered about the who until I ran into Whip on my way in tonight. He told me that Grace spent the afternoon here."

"Working with Dusty."

"After a passionate lunch here at the farmhouse?"

Tom decided a change of subject was in order. "Where'd you get that shrimp anyway? Is it fresh?"

"Fresh frozen. I had a real craving for shrimp tacos, checked the market in town, and voila! Now, back to our discussion."

"There is no discussion. I'm going to take a shower. Be back to help in a bit."

After a hasty but delicious meal, brother and sister hopped in

Tom's truck. As they drove to the community center for Scrabble night, Bella turned to him. "Sorry if I teased before."

"You won't be the only one."

"What's that mean?"

Tom gave her a brief summary of the incident in the barn, which prompted a spate of giggles. "Oh boy, those guys are brutal, aren't they?"

"Yup."

"I'm happy for you, brother. Grace is great."

"Yes, she is."

"You like her, don't you?"

He nodded, looking straight ahead. "Yup."

"A lot?"

"Yup."

"Well, here we go!" she said as Tom parked in the Community Center lot. "My first night of Scrabble in Saguaro. I love Scrabble!"

CHAPTER 20

When Tom and Bella walked in, the room was buzzing with the usual activity, with people setting up chairs and tables, unpacking and laying out the Scrabble boards and organizing the refreshment table. The latter consisted of simple fare—coffee, hot water and teas, juices, water, and plates of cookies, brownies, and whatever desserts members had brought to share. Tom nodded to Aria Firorelli, who had just set down a platter of her lemon squares and madeleines. Tom scanned the room and finally spied Grace, her back to them, talking with Pat Wordell, a spry seventy-something who was one of the founders of the club and an avid horsewoman. Pat boarded her horse at the Morgan's Run stables, but she had been talking with Harley about purchasing a second horse to keep at Valley Stables, maybe even a thoroughbred.

"Wow, this is quite a group, isn't it?" Bella said.

"Yup, they usually have twenty to thirty players, sometimes more. Hey, Brendan!" he called, waving to Brendan Stadler, one of the wranglers from Morgan's Run. Of medium height, with sandy hair and turquoise-blue eyes, the thirty-four-year-old cowboy paused, four folding chairs in his arms.

"Hey, Tom." His gaze moved to the woman beside him.

"Don't know if you've met my sister, Bella?"

Brendan grinned, leaning the chairs in his right hand against his leg and extending his hand to Bella. "Saw you from across the room at Harley and Ruthie's last week. Nice to finally meet you."

Tom smiled, standing back, watching the sparks ricochet back and forth between the two. "Can we help with those?" he asked.

"Won't say no," the other man replied. "There's a stack of them still in the closet."

It wasn't until they began drawing names from a hat to assign tables that Tom caught up Grace to say hello. Bella had attached herself to Brendan, and the two were in animated conversation near the refreshment table. Grace was chatting with the Valley Chorus director, Chuck Harvey, and his partner, George Ramos. Clearly in her element, she was laughing, sharing a joke with the portly conductor and his waiflike partner. She looked up and met Tom's eyes, waving.

"Excuse me," she said, stepping away from her companions and heading toward Tom.

"Hi."

She looking pretty and fresh-faced in skinny jeans, a beige sweater, and sneakers. Tom's body burned for her as they exchanged a friendly hug. "Hey."

She stepped back, face flushed. "So glad Bella came."

"She's crazy about board games, especially Scrabble, and as you can see, she's already found a cowboy."

"We're about to start. Good luck!"

"You too."

"Hmm..." Bella said, hip bumping against his. "Surprised you guys could control yourselves the way you were looking at each other. There was enough heat between you to start a forest fire."

"Ha-ha," he said, pointing to their left. "They've assigned you to that table. Good luck."

The evening was lively as they played, rotated tables, and chatted during the breaks, so Tom and Grace only saw each other from across a table. They shared the same game once, but aside from the occasional footsy, they concentrated on Scrabble.

At the end of the night, Brendan found brother and sister by the door. "Hey, do you need a ride home?" he asked, directing his question to Bella.

"Thanks, but I came with Tom, and I've got a really early wake-up tomorrow."

As her brother walked off to say goodbye to Grace, Brendan said, "It was great to meet you. Maybe we could grab a coffee or burger sometime?"

She smiled. "I'd like that. Got your phone?" He handed it to her, and she punched in some numbers and handed it back. "Now you've got my number. Give me a call."

"Will do. Night."

"Night," she said, turning back to the room, where she spied Tom and Grace embracing. *Hmm... That's a red-hot romance if ever I've seen one.*

❧

TOM HELD HER LONGER THAN WAS ENTIRELY APPROPRIATE FOR A Scrabble-night goodbye. "I'll be in Sonoita all day tomorrow, checking out some horses. We may stay the night, so I probably won't see you till Friday night."

"I'm looking forward to that," she said softly, taking a step back, noticing several curious eyes watching them. "I'll be out with Nick tomorrow, but my dad's got some kind of dental procedure Friday, so I have to be at the store."

"No worries. Whatever time you can give Dusty is great."

"Good night, then," she said.

"Night," he said, giving her a warm smile.

❧

"SO?" BELLA ASKED AS THEY DROVE HOME.

"So what?"

"So when you gonna see her again, hmm?"

"Not that it's any of your business, sister dear, but Friday."

"Ooh... Are you taking her someplace special?"

"The Red Mesa. It's northwest of here. Great place. I'll take you there sometime soon, or maybe Brendan will?" Eyes on the road, Tom grinned.

"He's pretty cute, isn't he? More of a fries-and-burgers guy, though, I'm guessing."

Her brother laughed. "You never know. People have hidden depths."

"Hmph. After my track record with men, I'm not getting too excited. I gave him my number. Ball's in his court."

"Lucky him," Tom said, receiving a punch in the arm.

Like lovestruck fools, both grinned as they drove north in the inky darkness of the Gila Highway.

CHAPTER 21

Friday morning, Grace placed her father's scrambled eggs and bacon in front of him, setting his rack of toast in the middle of the table along with strawberry jam and butter. "More coffee, Papa?"

"Thanks, honey, I'm fine. Sit for a minute, will you?"

She sat across from him, taking a sip of her tea. "You okay?"

"Fit as a fiddle. You remember about my dentist appointment this afternoon?"

She nodded.

"They're pulling a tooth and will give me a pretty good shot of Novocain."

She smiled at him. "I should hope so."

"Are you okay lockin' up tonight? I think I'll wanna come home and rest after, if that's okay?"

"Of course. Are Paulo and Joe working all day?"

"Paulo, yes, but I let the Davis kid go yesterday while you were out at the Stables. You ran out to your singing so quick that I didn't get a chance to tell you last night."

"What reason did you give?" she asked, breathing a sigh of relief that she wouldn't have to work alongside the sulky young man.

"Said we were fine with you, me, and Paulo for now. Gave him two weeks' wages."

"How'd he take it?"

"Didn't say much, but I could tell he was angry. He impresses me as an angry kid in general, so who knows. I'm only tellin' you in case you see him around town. Paulo seemed to think he was planning to head back to Yuma soon anyway."

"So yesterday was his last day?"

Her father nodded. "Yup."

"Honestly, I'm glad," she said, rubbing her arms as a chill came over her. "He kind of gave me the creeps."

"Me too. Now, we'd better hustle. One of us has to be there to open on time."

"I'll go, Papa. Finish your breakfast. You can leave everything, and I'll clean up at lunch."

"Thanks, sweetie. Sometime soon, we'll have to sit down, and you can tell me all about your horse whispering. I know, I know, not tonight 'cause it's your big date, but I'd really like to hear about it."

"And maybe someday soon, you can come out to meet Dusty," she said, hugging him from behind, then grabbing her backpack. "See you in a few."

THE DAY SPED BY IN A FLURRY OF ACTIVITY. FRIDAYS WERE ALWAYS BUSY, and this one was no exception. Paulo did all the heavy lifting and mostly stayed back in the yards and store rooms. Unlike Joe, who had taken every opportunity for a cigarette break during his four days with them, Paulo was a quiet, steady worker. Wilbur left at three thirty for his appointment, and Grace worked the front of the store while Paulo cleaned and straightened things up in the back.

At five, he emerged, his backpack and jacket over one shoulder. "Need anything before I go?" he asked, finding Grace taking in the signs and merchandise they put out on the sidewalk each day.

Grace smiled. "Thanks, Paulo, but this is the last of it, then I'm heading out too. Here, this for you," she said, handing him an envelope with his week's wages.

"Thanks. See you in the morning, then."

"Night," she said, going to lock the front door behind him.

After emptying the cash register, she stored the money in the safe. Her father would reconcile everything Sunday and drop in the bank deposit drawer that night. As she locked the safe, she heard a sound, like scuffling, coming from the storerooms. They often had rats and mice, and she wondered if she should set a trap or two before she went home. Suddenly, she heard another sound, much clearer. *Footsteps.*

"Hey, Papa, is that you?" she called.

She grabbed her backpack and headed toward the back door, switching lights off as she proceeded. As she rounded the corner, he stepped out of the darkness to the side of the door.

"Joe! You startled me. What are you doing here? Paulo's already gone home."

"What do you care?" he mumbled, eyes flashing fire.

Heart in her throat, Grace stood up straighter. "You shouldn't be here. Please go."

"Yeah? Who's gonna make me? Your old man thinks he can give me the shaft after four days? Well, fuck that."

Grace fumbled in her back pocket and pulled out her phone, pressing the button for her most recent call, praying it was someone she knew. "I'm going to ask you to leave one more time, and then I'm calling Sheriff Boone." As she spoke, she heard a faint voice talking. Tom. "Grace, is that you?" Tom asked, his voice comforting as she backed away from the glowering man.

"What the hell are you doing there, bitch?" Joe said, coming closer.

He cornered her with no way for her to get around him. She could smell his breath—a sour mixture of alcohol and tobacco. "Stay away from me! My dad's in the house! He's probably already called the sheriff and—"

Before she could duck, his left arm swung out, catching her right cheek, knocking her to the floor. The phone skittered out of her hands and under a storage cabinet. Stunned for an instant, she came to her senses and started screaming, "Help, help! Tom, he's in the store! Call the sheriff! Call my dad!"

Davis grabbed her shirt and dragged her into the grain room. Grace kicked and screamed, clawing at the floorboards, attempting to get away.

"Stop it, bitch!" he growled. "This'll be much easier if you chill, get it?" He began tearing at her clothes, slapping her, grabbing her breasts and ripping her jeans.

Grace continued her screaming and kicking. His rough, grimy hands tore her jeans, yanking them down, then shredding her panties as he threw them aside. Grace landed a solid blow to his neck, allowing her to scoot back out of his grasp for an instant. The rough floor scratched her skin, leaving splinters and a blood trail. Her kick had stunned him, but not for long. Joe crawled on all fours, catching her before she reached the door.

"Now you've had it, bitch," he said. His fist came down, and everything went black.

~

EXCITED ABOUT THEIR DINNER AT RED MESA, TOM HAD BEEN HEADED for the shower when the call from Grace came in. He grabbed the truck keys and ran out the door, meeting Bella in the driveway.

"Hey, Tom, what's wrong?" she asked, staring at him in horror.

"Grace is in trouble. Someone's at the store. Gotta call her dad and the sheriff."

Bella ran beside him to the truck and hopped into the passenger seat. "I'm coming."

As they hurtled down the road toward town, Tom barked, "Call 911 and tell the sheriff to get over to Valley Hardware immediately."

As she dialed, Bella said, "Who are you calling?"

"Wilbur McGraw, I hope," he said. A few seconds later, he said, "Wilbur, thank God. Grace is in trouble. Someone's in the store!"

Wilbur clicked off, grabbed a bat he kept by the back door, and hurried out in his stocking feet.

GRACE CAME TO AND GAGGED. JOE'S FOUL, FETID BREATH SURROUNDED her as he licked and bit her neck, at the same time yanking his own jeans down. Her head felt as if it were about to explode. He'd pinned her down and spread her legs. Knowing what was coming, she groped around the floor with her one free hand until she grabbed hold of a small spade and swung it at his head.

"Gimme that, cunt!" He wrested it from her, then twisted her hand behind her. "You're gonna get what's coming to you and your miserable old fuck of a father."

Grace struggled, but it was no use. He was stronger, and she was dizzy and sick from the beating. She closed her eyes, wet with tears, and prayed. Suddenly, she heard a thud and Davis fell on top of her. Then everything went black again.

Wilbur kicked the lifeless body aside, discarding the baseball bat as he reached down and cradled his precious daughter in his arms. "You're safe now, sweetie."

He lifted her up and carried her into the storeroom. After setting her down, he removed his shirt and wrapped it around her naked, bruised body. Shouts and banging behind them heralded the arrival of Sheriff Boone and two of his men.

"Scum is in there," Wilbur called. "We need a doctor. Now."

"Chester's on his way," Boone said, directing his men to the grain room.

As they hauled a handcuffed, half-conscious Davis out the back door, Tom's truck screeched to a halt in the drive. "Where is she? Is she okay?"

"She's okay, but probably wouldn't want you to see her just now," Boone said. "The doc's on his way."

Tom ignored the sheriff and ran to the door just as Bella caught up. "He's right, Tommy. Better that we stay out until the doctor gets here."

"No way," he said, pushing by her.

CHAPTER 22

The scene in the storeroom broke Tom's heart. Wilbur rocked his daughter, cradling her bruised and battered body, tears streaming down his face. Grace's right eye was swollen shut, her left cheek black and blue. An ugly red gash ran from her lips to her chin, her mouth bloody and swollen.

"Jesus, Wilbur," Tom said, crouching beside them.

"Look what that bastard did to my baby," he sobbed, holding her closer. Grace winced then tried to sit up.

Tom reached out, taking her hand. "Try not to move, baby. Doc's on his way."

"Too tight, Papa," she whispered through swollen lips.

"So sorry, baby." Wilbur looked up at Tom. "I like to run to the house and get her some clothes. Bastard ripped hers to shreds. Could you hold her for a few minutes?"

In answer, Tom slid across the floor and held out his arms. Gently, he took her from Wilbur, careful not to hold on too tightly.

"I'll be back soon," Wilbur said, hurrying from the room.

Grace relaxed against his chest and sighed before passing out a third time.

Tom wondered if he should call Bella to look her over, but decided it was better to wait for the town physician, Chester Black, whose home and office were less than a mile away. She shivered, so he shrugged out of his jacket and laid it over her, leaning down to kiss her forehead. "I'm so sorry. My sweet, beautiful Grace."

She startled, and her eyes fluttered open. "Tom, is that you?" She grasped his forearm.

"I'm right here, sweetheart. I'm not going anywhere."

As she closed her eyes and drifted off, he held her close and whispered, "I love you so much. Please stay with me. I can't live without you."

Commotion in the hall startled him, and he looked up to spy Chester Black and Bella right behind him. Chester looked down at them, shaking his head. "Does it look like she has broken bones?"

"Can't tell," Tom replied. "We haven't moved her, although I think her dad brought her in here from the grain room...where it happened. There's a blood trail."

"I'd like to get her into the house and into bed, but I'd like to look her over first. She may be better off in the hospital. Your sister has kindly offered to assist me, so if you can lay her flat, we'll take over."

"I'll lay her flat, but I'm not leaving her."

"Tom, I know you care for this woman, but I guarantee she wouldn't want you to be here for this. Set her down and let us examine her. Now. I don't want to ask the sheriff to step in, but I will if you don't leave the room."

"It'll be okay," Bella said, massaging her brother's shoulder. "We'll take really good care of her."

Tom left the room, intending to wait in the hall, but the sheriff's men led him to the front of the store and instructed him to remain there. Sheriff Boone found him sitting dejectedly by the counter. "We've got a forensic team coming to process the back. Better for you to stay here. Her dad'll be in soon to wait with you."

A half hour later, Wilbur and Tom looked up as the physician came into the room. "No broken bones, just a lot of bruising and a mild concussion. She needs a couple of stitches in her lip, which I can do, but I think she's better off getting into her own bed first. Bella will clean her up, and then I can do the stitches. We could order a stretcher, but it's safe for someone to carry her. Sheriff's guys could do it, but—"

Tom shot out of his seat. "I'll take her in."

Chester gave him a warm smile. "I was hoping you'd volunteer. And guys," he said, gazing from one to the other of them. "She's looks pretty bad, but she's gonna be fine."

Wilbur stood, his eyes fixed on the doctor. "Was she... I mean, did he...?"

"Thankfully, there was no violation in the way you're thinking. You got to her just in time, but I would still consider this sexual assault. A very violent, traumatic sexual assault. Gonna take some healing."

The men nodded as they followed him back to the storeroom. Grace was dressed in flannel pajama bottoms and a sweatshirt. Her face was clean of blood, a temporary bandage over the gash. Bella held two ice packs up on either side of her face, but stood aside as the men entered, packing the ice packs and her equipment in her bag.

As Tom lifted her, Grace moaned. "It's okay, baby. We'll have you in bed soon." She felt impossibly frail and small as he made his way out of the store toward the house. Finally, he laid her gently on her bed, now covered with towels. "There you go, baby," he whispered, kissing her forehead before he straightened up.

"Thanks, son," Chester said. "We'll need some time now to get her cleaned up and stitched."

"Don't worry," Bella said, giving Tom a quick hug, then closing the door leaving him alone in the empty hallway.

He could hear voices downstairs—neighbors come to support Wilbur -- but he remained where he was, a sentry at the door of his beloved.

~

AFTER WHAT SEEMED AN ETERNITY, THE BEDROOM DOOR OPENED, AND Bella stepped out. "All set. She's had a sponge bath, has been stitched up, and is ready to sleep. She's asking for you."

Tom stepped in to find the doctor packing up and Grace propped up in her bed. Bella had washed her body and her hair, drying and combing it gently. She now wore what appeared to be a nightgown, soft jersey material covered with tiny blue flowers. She held an ice pack over her right eye, which she set beside her as he approached. "Some date, huh?" she asked, managing a crooked smile that caused her to wince. "Did you remember to call the Red Mesa and cancel?"

"No, but I'm sure they'll understand," he said, pulling a chair to the side of the bed. He reached to take her hand, cold and clammy from the ice pack. "How're you doing?"

"I think Dr. Black has me pretty drugged up, so not too bad." Her face registered pain as she attempted to smile.

"No more grinning," he said.

Chester cleared his throat. "She's going to need someone to stay with her tonight. Your sister has volunteered, but she's on call for a birth, so I'm not sure that's the best solution."

"Does it need to be a medical person?" Tom asked as Bella stepped back into the room.

"No, just someone to wake her maybe once during the night. Some docs wouldn't bother with this, but I like to be cautious."

"I'll stay. I want to stay," Tom said. "You go home, Bella. I've got this."

"You sure? I can reach my attending and try to get someone else to relieve my on call," Bella said.

"I'm fine. I'll call Harley and Whip. They'll alert the guys if I'm late tomorrow."

The doctor spent a few minutes talking about signs to look out for and the meds and ice treatments he recommended, then headed off with a "Good luck. She's going to be fine. What she'll need now is rest and loving support. Her father too."

Tom asked Bella to stay with Grace long enough for him to check on Wilbur, who appeared to have calmed himself with the bottle. His neighbors assured Tom that they'd get him some food and make sure he got to bed. They also said they'd take care of the store one way or the other in the morning.

Tom left his boots by the back door, then headed back upstairs. He gave Bella his truck keys and hugged her good night, then washed up in Grace's bathroom. Grace was sleeping when he returned, so he set his watch alarm, shut off the light, and carefully lay down on the bed beside her. He pulled a quilt over both of them, found her hand, and brought it to his lips. "Night, my sweet girl. I love you."

CHAPTER 23

"Thank you for staying with me," Grace said as she emerged from the bathroom fully dressed to find Tom straightening the bed.

"Morning," he said. "You want to get back under the covers?"

She shook her head. "I've got to get to the store. What time is it?"

"Six fifteen," he said, giving her a look. "And no one expects you to work today."

"Well, I'm not lying around here," she said, wincing as she sat to put on her shoes.

"Grace, be sensible," he said, coming to crouch beside her, hand on her knee." You can't go anywhere. The doc's coming in an hour to check you over, and you need to rest and heal."

She moved her leg, pulling away from his touch. "I need to work and do normal things, not sit around and dwell on last night."

He took her hand, but she wriggled out of his grasp. "I've gotta go home and get cleaned up. I'll come right back, but promise me you won't go out of this house until Dr. Black checks you over."

She gazed down at him, one eye still swollen shut, both black and blue. "Tom, I am so grateful to you for last night, but I'm fine. Please don't fuss over me. I'll wait for Chester, then if he says it's okay, I'm going to the store. You go home. I'm sure they need you at the stables."

"I'm not leaving you alone. Your dad's opening late, waiting till I get back."

"This is ridiculous," she said, swaying as she stood up, her head spinning.

"You getting out of bed is more ridiculous," he said, following her as she descended the stairs, gripping the handrail.

Her father had made breakfast and was sitting at the table as they came in. "Morning, honey. I heard you moving around, so I whipped up some eggs. Sit."

"Thanks, Papa." She gave him a crooked smile and slowly lowered herself into her chair.

Tom watched the older man's face reflecting his own concern. *What the hell are we going to do here?* he thought as the phone rang.

Wilbur rose and answered it. "Hey, Chuck," he said. "How're you doing?" There was a short pause, then he said, "She's doing okay. Doc's coming soon. Tryin' to convince her to stay home."

Another pause.

"You sure? That'd be real helpful. I know we'd all appreciate it. Thanks. See you soon."

Wilbur hung up, exchanged a look with Tom, then gave a sidelong glance to his daughter before he sat down.

"What did Chuck want?" she asked, eyeing him.

"He's offered to come visit for the day."

She stared at him, mouth open in surprise. "How did he find out?"

"Now, now, honey. Don't go getting' upset. He saw one of the sheriff's guys at the Café this morning."

"He needn't come. I won't have it. Call him back."

Tom leaned forward trying to take her hand, which she planted firmly in her lap out of reach. "Think about it, Grace, will you? It'd be nice to have Chuck for company."

"I am not an invalid and will not be treated like one. Papa, call him back."

"No."

Surprised at his tone, they both stared at him. Wilbur had crossed his arms over his barrel chest, jaw set. "Don't say another word. He's comin' and he's stayin' all day until I get home. You are also not allowed to set foot in the store." As Grace opened her mouth to speak, he raised his hand in protest. "Nope, not another word. It's settled. I've got to get over there and open up."

"But—"

"But nothing. Paulo's probably out front waiting."

She blanched, her swollen lips trembling.

"He's already phoned. He feels responsible and offered to quit. I said we'd talk this morning. If it'll be too hard for you to have him there, I'll let him go with a month's pay."

Grace shook her head. "Of course not. It wasn't his fault."

As her father grabbed his jacket, he turned. "Give it some thought, honey. We'll talk tonight." He kissed the top of her head, nodded to Tom, then headed out.

When the door closed behind Wilbur, Tom looked over. "You okay?"

"No, I am not okay. I look like the loser in a prize fight. I'm being treated like I'm on death's door by everyone around me, and all I want to do is get back to my life."

"Grace, you've had an incredibly traumatizing experience. You're hurting, and you need rest. People just want to help you."

She was about to speak, but was interrupted by a knock at the front door. Tom left the room and returned with Chester Black. "Morning, Grace. Glad to see you having a good breakfast."

"Hello," she answered, gazing up at him.

"How're you feeling?"

"Smothered."

"Excuse me?" he said.

"I've got people orchestrating my every move, making all my decisions, treating me like an invalid." She waved at Tom. "And I have a pounding headache."

"You have a concussion. Headache's normal. How did you sleep?"

The lanky, physician with thick salt-and-pepper hair, bushy eyebrows, and twinkling coal-black eyes sat down across from her.

"Okay."

Black looked over at Tom. "Everything okay from your observations?"

Tom nodded.

"Any trouble rousing her?"

"No, she woke up just fine."

"Good. I'd like to check you over after breakfast, if that's okay?"

"You can go," Grace said, looking over at Tom. "I'll be fine."

"Wait," Chester said. "Are you the only other person in the house?"

Before Tom could reply, she said, "My father is ten steps away at the store."

"I don't want you to be alone today. Not until you're a bit steadier."

"She has a friend coming soon," Tom replied. "I can stay till then."

"Good."

"This is crazy," Grace said, tears of frustration rimming her eyes.

The kindly physician came around the table and sat beside her, opening his bag. "I know this is hard, but you've had a pretty serious assault to your body and head. If someone can't stay with you, I'd feel better transferring you to Grenville Hospital for observation," he said, raising his otoscope to check her eyes.

Tom watched her shoulders droop, the picture of dejection, and his heart ached. If Joe Davis stepped in the door at that moment, he was pretty certain he would beat him to death.

CHAPTER 24

Once back at work, Grace drifted through the days in a semi trance. Sore and tired, she felt her heart pound every time she heard a noise from the rear of the store. Paulo had apologized a dozen times since her return to work on Monday, and she'd assured him she was okay. Her father hired a local kid, Paul Shea, two days after the assault. Paul had taken a year off from University of Arizona and was only too happy for the work. Strong as an ox, freckle-faced, with red hair and rosy cheeks, Paul proved to be a warm, welcome presence.

Tom called several times a day and had stopped in briefly when he was in town Wednesday. She had brushed him off, insisting she was fine but would rather not see people, including him, until she felt more ready to be in public. Curious villagers who had all heard of the attack stopped by the store. After a quick hello, Grace would duck back into the office to escape the gawking. On Thursday, she was hiding out in the early afternoon when her cell rang.

"Hey," Tom said. "How are you doing?"

"I'm in the office trying to avoid being the star in a freak show."

"Aw, baby, I'm sorry."

"Everyone's sorry, that's the problem. I'm tired of it."

"I wondered if you'd like to have that dinner tomorrow at the Red Mesa?"

"I don't know. The way I look and all."

"It's out of town, people won't know you, and the swelling's gone down. Your bruises are fading, aren't they?"

"Thanks, to Arnica, the miracle cream. I don't know about dinner, though. Aside from my appearance, my jaw hurts when I chew and—"

"My house, then? I'll cook. Soup?"

"No!" she replied a bit more abruptly than she'd intended. "Okay. Red Mesa it is. I'll buy some heavy makeup and see what I can do."

A few minutes later, she hung up, went home, and crumbled into a fetal position on the living room sofa. *How can I see him, be with him, when his touch makes me nauseous?* The thought of any man's touch sent shivers of fear through her frail body. She'd lost ten pounds in the past week and could barely hold down a bite of food. Grace sighed. *At least it's better to go to a restaurant than his house. Safer.*

❧

THERE WAS SOMETHING IN HER VOICE THAT SCARED TOM. HE swallowed hard as they made arrangements, then said goodbye.

Bella came into the kitchen and took one look at him. "What's wrong?"

"It's Grace. She's in a bad place, and she's shut me out."

"That's totally normal after an experience like she's had. Give her time. She might want to try to see someone, a therapist, you know? I hear Haley Alvarez in town is terrific."

"Not my business." He threw his phone on the counter and started down to the lower paddocks.

"Don't you want your phone?" Bella called, then shook her head and headed off to work.

❧

"WATCH OUT, BEACHED WHALE COMING THROUGH," RUTHIE MORGAN Langdon said as she waddled into the examination room. "How can I look like this at eight months and my gorgeous sister-in-law barely looks pregnant?"

Bella smiled at the youngest Morgan sibling, her curly red-blonde hair tied back in a loose ponytail, ruddy freckled face smudged after a day in the fields, her belly straining the front of dust-covered overalls.

"Everyone carries their babies differently."

"And some people look more beautiful pregnant. Not me, but some people."

Bella chuckled. "How are you feeling?"

"Okay, just fat."

"Where's Charlotte today?"

"At the Big House," she said, referring to the elder Morgans' home at the center of the Morgan's Run ranch. "Mom picked her up from day care."

After the examination, the women chatted for a while in Bella's office. As Ruthie rose to leave, she said, "Are you enjoying living out at Valley Stables?"

"Very much. It's beautiful."

"Yup. Must be nice to realize your dream at our dad's and Spark's time of life."

"Sounds like they worked hard for a lot of years to achieve it."

"Yes, they did. How's your handsome brother doing?"

"Loves the job. He's worried about Grace, but otherwise, same ole same ole."

"They've been seeing a lot of each other, huh? Good for both of them."

Bella nodded. "He's crazy about her."

"When I heard about the attack, I wanted to rush right over, but then I thought I should give her space. I'll pop over soon. Horrible. Dad says they charged the monster and will probably send him over to Florence rather than holding him here."

"He's certainly left a shattered young woman in his wake."

"Poor baby. Anything we can do?"

"I know you guys are good friends. I'm sure she'd love to see you. I think when she heals physically, she should see someone, to help with the trauma. Has to be her decision, though."

The two women hugged. As Ruthie turned to go, Bella said, "And for the record, you look just as beautiful as your sister-in-law."

"Yeah, right," Ruthie said, "but I love you for saying it."

CHAPTER 25

"You look completely lovely," Tom said as the waiter stepped away to get their drinks. The Red Mesa glowed with candlelight and the spectacular colors of the setting sun. They sat by the window gazing west over the terrace, gardens, and mountains beyond. Grace wore a blue dress with embroidered velvet accents. While lovely, it looked two sizes too big after her recent weight loss.

"Thank you. This is an incredible place."

He had already asked how she was, so he dared not broach the subject again. "It is pretty great, isn't it?" He reached across the table intending to take her hand, but she slid it out of reach into her lap.

"I'm sorry Tom. I can't... Being touched. It's... I can't."

"It's okay, baby. I understand."

"No, you don't, and please don't call me baby."

Sadness overwhelmed him as Tom gazed at the woman he loved. *Will she ever come back to me?* "I'm sorry. Just tell me what you need, and I'll do it."

"This was a mistake," she said shaking her head. "I agreed because it seemed safer than coming to your house. I can't... I need time."

Oscar, their waiter, appeared and set down Grace's wine and

Tom's beer. "Have you decided on dinner?" he asked, readying his pad.

Tom smiled up at him. "You know what, Oscar? We need just a few more minutes, okay?"

The waiter bowed. "Of course, sir."

Alone again, Tom watched as she lifted her wine to her lips with a trembling hand, her eyes gazing down at the table. "Would you rather not stay? I'll do whatever makes you feel safe, ba— Grace."

She nodded. "I want to go home."

Tom set down his beer and stood. "Be right back. You okay here for a minute?"

She nodded.

He crossed the room and found Oscar in the next dining room. After his explanation that they needed to leave, the waiter directed him to the bar.

"No problem at all, sir."

Tom settled the check with a generous tip for Oscar and returned to the table to find Grace shivering and miserable.

He longed to take her in his arms, but he knew such an overture would be rebuffed or worse. "All set?"

Grace stood, her legs threatening to buckle beneath her. As Tom moved to help her, she shot out her hand to keep him at bay, grasping her chair for support. He pretended not to notice the shakiness and stepped back, giving her space while remaining vigilant should she falter.

They were silent on the way back to town. As he drove down Main Street, he said, "You hungry? I could get takeout from Gracie's or the Bulldog?"

"Thanks, but I'd rather just go home. I can find something."

Yeah, right, he thought, but didn't reply.

As he parked, he expected her to bolt without a word, but instead, she sighed as he switched off the ignition. "Tom, I think we should take a break... Seeing each other, I mean. I care for you, I really do, but I'm empty inside. Numb."

"I'll do whatever you want, but don't you think loving support might help you to heal?"

"I don't know... I've been able to work. Maybe as the scars fade and I get further from that night, the rest will be easier."

The rest meaning having anything to do with me? he thought. "Dusty misses you."

"I miss him. Could I come over this weekend? Maybe just to say hello?"

"What day were you thinking? I'd need to be with you or call Nick or one of the guys."

"Sunday afternoon? Two-ish?"

"You got it."

"Thanks for bringing me home. The Red Mesa is amazing."

"We can go again when you're feeling better." His body burned for her touch as he hopped out and came to open her door. After unlocking the front door, she stepped inside. "Night, Tom."

"Night, Grace."

As the door closed behind her, his heart ached with loneliness.

CHAPTER 26

Ripped up inside, Tom threw himself into work at the stables. Just before Grace was scheduled to arrive Sunday, he was called up to the track so didn't see her. When he returned to help bring the mustangs in, he asked Whip how it had gone with Dusty.

"Weirdest thing, boss. She patted him for a few minutes, then said thanks and took off. Poor Dusty was so happy to see her. Poor guy whinnied and snorted for half an hour after she left."

"Not surprised."

"She seems like a different person."

"She is. Gonna take time, I guess."

"They charge the guy?"

"Apparently."

"Geez."

"Geez is right. Bastard should be strung up," Tom said, kicking a bucket next to the barn door and startling the mare walking beside him.

"Why don't you head home, boss? The guys and I can finish bringing 'em in."

"Thanks, Whip, but I'd rather keep busy."

As he walked home in the growing twilight, Tom gazed up at the sky full of stars and wondered whether he'd ever be happy again.

From heaven to hell, he mused as a nighthawk's cries pierced the silence.

When he reached the back porch, he spied a lone figure sitting on the steps and was surprised to find Harley, beer in hand, waiting. "Hey, what are you doing out here, boss? Shouldn't you be home with the family?"

"Had a few minutes. Thought I'd check in."

"Lemme grab a beer and I'll be right out, unless you'd rather come inside?"

"Nice night. I'm happy."

Two minutes later, Tom sat beside him and took his first swig of Desert Amber. "I needed that," he sighed. "How was everything after I left?"

"Okay, although Princess Alice is giving Rupert a run for his money." He referred to jockeys Alice Hanley and Rupert Mann. She'd been hired first and never let her fellow jockey forget it. "What a prima donna. She won't accept anyone unless they're incompetent. Afraid they'll make her look bad. We spent all day refereeing. It's exhausting."

"Want me to talk to her?"

"Naw, that's my job. I just wasn't up for a hissy fit today. In fact, she wasn't supposed to be here at all. Rupert was working with Leo. It wasn't any of her damn business."

"So...anything on your mind except the temperamental Ms. Hanley?"

Harley grinned, raising an eyebrow as he looked over at him. "The first is easy. My best friend is trying to pressure me into going on a pack trip, and I can't if I want to stay married. Ruthie looks like she's dropping the baby any minute, and we'll be away a week. He's got Nick Parker, but Jeb can't go, and Ruthie, of course, is unavailable. Robbie sometimes goes, but he's swamped running other trips. I suggested Whip, but Ben thinks they'd eat him alive."

"What about me? That's what you're after, right? I mean, what's gonna prevent them from devouring me?"

"Ben thinks Kitteridge is a flake, but that people listen to you."

Tom grinned. "Whip may be a flake, but he's a very competent flake and he's a much better rider than I am."

"In a rodeo, maybe. Out on the trail, I'd take you every day of the week and twice on Sunday."

"What about the mustangs and things up the hill?"

"We're fine. Whip can supervise things down here and I'll beg Maggie to let go of Parker for at least a day or two."

Tom thought about the past week and shrugged. "Why not? If you think things are okay here, I'm game. Where are we going?"

"I think they're riding to Faulkner's Ridge through the Painted Valley. Can't remember, have you been out there?"

"The valley, but never been on the ridge. 'Sposed to be pretty."

"'Tis that, but some of it can be tricky. It's not rainy season, so you should be fine. They'll descend from the ridge on a different path to avoid the area where we almost lost Kyle Morgan. Inexperienced, idiot rider. Not him, one of the guests. I think Ben plans to spend more time in the valley first to make up for the shortened time on the Ridge."

"Okay, I'm game. Should I call him or will you?" Tom asked.

"Thanks, I'll let him know."

"So what was the other thing you wanted?"

"Ruthie tells me your girl is a mess."

"She's pretty messed up, but she's had a major trauma. I'm giving her space."

"Is that wise? I should think she'd need you at a time like this. Then again, what I know about women could fit on the point of a pin."

Tom laughed. "What're you talking about? You live with three of 'em."

"Babies don't count, Willow's never given me an ounce of trouble, and I've known Ruthie all my life and will never figure her out."

"Well, maybe a week away will give Grace some healing time, and I'll be out of cell phone range so I can't pester her."

Harley shrugged. "Your call, but you've just made Ben Morgan very happy. Thanks for the beer."

"Night, boss," Tom said as Harley rounded the side of the house, waving over his shoulder as he headed for his truck.

Maybe a week away will be good for both of us, if there ever is a both of us in the future, he thought, warming up to the idea of getting out of town. Grace had stopped answering his calls, and her phone went right to voicemail. *Let her come to you, buddy, if she ever does.*

GRACE WEPT ALL THE WAY BACK TO TOWN AFTER LEAVING DUSTY. THE decision to go out to the

Stables had been difficult because she dreaded seeing Tom. Then when she arrived to find him gone, a pang of sadness had lodged itself in her chest. Even seeing Dusty hadn't calmed her roiling emotions as it usually did. As she petted the strong, steady creature from the other side of the fence, dueling emotions of sadness at not seeing Tom and the anxiety about what she would do if he appeared overwhelmed her. After a few minutes, she had kissed Dusty's nose and hurried to her car, speeding out of the stables property much faster than she should have.

What am I going to do? she wondered through her tears. *I miss him and love him more than life itself, but the thought of his touch terrifies me. How can I feel this way about the man I adore?*

DAILY ROUTINES HAD BEEN SMOOTHER, AND HER BODY HEALED. SHE'D settled back in at the store, and as her scars and bruises faded, people's curiosity did too. Paulo and Paul, or "Paul and Paul," as customers called them, worked harmoniously together and had been a huge help. Their presence gave her time to take care of a backlog of projects and paperwork, and the two strong young men lightened her father's load considerably. She thought about Tom every minute of the day and night, but still did not pick up when he called and knew she wasn't ready to see him. *Will I ever be?* she mused Tuesday evening as she closed up.

Paul worked from noon to six and always stayed until she closed up so she wouldn't be alone. "Night, Grace," he said as they walked out together. "See you tomorrow."

"Thanks, Paul. You are such a godsend to us right now. I hope you realize that."

The young man smiled. "You take care, now." As per her father's instructions, he stood in the parking lot, watching until she reached her back door and waved to him. Only then did he head to his bike parked in the shade by the back of the store.

CHAPTER 27

"My least favorite thing—schmoozing," Tom said as he and Bella drove to Morgan's Run.

"I'm excited," she said. "I haven't seen the Lodge, and I hear it's spectacular."

"What Morgan property isn't?"

As they drove up and parked, Bella oohed and aahed at the beautiful three-story adobe structure. "Wow! So much more than even my imagination conjured up!"

The party was in full swing as they came into the main hall. "Welcome," Ben Senior said. "We're so grateful to you, Tom. Wish we could have found someone else and spared my son Ben as well. Maggie's worried sick something will happen while he's away."

"She's got a terrific support system," Bella said as the Morgan patriarch gave her a hug.

"Yes, she does. My Nora has been nagging her to move into the Big House with the kids while he's away."

"It's not my business," Bella said, "but it's not a bad idea. Means there's someone with the kids and someone to get her to the hospital."

"We'll keep workin' on her," he said, kind blue eyes gazing from brother to sister. "In the end it's gotta be Maggie's decision. Now, you two mingle while I find my bride."

Tom circulated, meeting each member of the pack trip. Most were experienced riders, which always made things easier. Milly Watkins, a Canadian film and television star, and her husband, Buddy Glen, owned a ranch in British Columbia and both were expert riders, as were their kids, Ursula and Donnie. Ursula's boyfriend, Sonny, had only ridden a few times, and the other couple, Milly's costar Patch Andrews and his much younger girlfriend, Sooky, had never been on a horse. They as well as Sonny had spent the past three days taking riding lessons from Jeb, Nick, and Brendan at the ranch's stables.

"Great to meet you, Tommy," Sookie said, flipping her blonde ponytail over her shoulder and striking a pose. Her black top and slacks appeared painted on, and she wore a fire-engine-red bolero jacket and six-inch heels. It looked to Tom as if the slightest movement might cause her top to burst open, setting her enormous breasts free.

"At last, a normal person," Sookie said. "I just met your sister Belle over there. She's cool too. Wish she was goin' on the trip instead of Ursula stick-up-her-ass and her greasy brother."

"It's Bella."

"Whatever." She sipped her Cosmo and gazed around the room. "I wish Nickie had come tonight."

"Probably getting all the gear ready. How'd your lessons go?"

"Okay, but I gotta tell you, if I have to go on this dumb cowboy trip —no offense—Nickie's riding beside me the whole way. In fact, if I freak out, I'm riding *with* him."

Poor Parker, Tom thought as Sookie's boyfriend, Patch, joined them. "Hey, babe, I'm turning in. We've got an early start tomorrow."

Sookie rolled her eyes, setting her drink on the table. She leaned in, winking as she whispered to Tom, "This is what happens when you hang around with an old geezer."

As Tom watched them head off, he guessed there to be a twenty-year age difference, minimum. He looked to be in his late forties, early fifties, while Sookie appeared to be closer to Ursula's age, early twenties.

They'll be lots of fun, he thought, heading over to say goodbye to Ben.

"Hey, buddy, you meet everyone?" the eldest Morgan brother asked, patting Tom's shoulder.

"I think so. Didn't say much to the Watkins woman, but talked to her husband and son for a while. Good thing they're all good riders. It'll make things a bit smoother."

"Yeah, but the daughter's a real prima donna. If I had to predict, I'd guess we'll want to throw her and Patch's bimbo girlfriend, Sookie 'I'm no cowgirl,' off a cliff halfway up Faulkner's Ridge."

Tom laughed. "Yeah, they're gonna be rough, but at least Ursula can ride. Sookie claims if she doesn't like it, she's riding with Parker."

Ben shook his head. "Over my dead body. You and Bella can take off if you want. This is winding down, and I need you out at Morgan's Run by five a.m."

"No worries. I'll be there," Tom said, heading across the room to collect Bella, who was chatting with Don Glen. "You ready, sis?"

"Sure am. Have a great trip, Donnie."

"Wish you were coming along," said the heavy-set twenty-something with dark hair and biceps that strained his flannel shirt.

"I can ride," she said, "but one or two days are my limit. Night."

As brother and sister left to drive home, she turned to him. "You've got your work cut out with that crew."

"Yup, but your boyfriend, Donnie, there, and his parents are really good riders, so at least we won't have all seven of 'em sliding off their horses into the sagebrush."

"*Not* my boyfriend. Cute, but way too full of himself and all the things he's so good at."

"Great."

"Still no word from Grace?"

"Nope."

"Have you tried to call her?"

"Yup."

"Are you gonna try again before you take off?"

"Nope. I'm giving her space. When I get back, I'll go by, but I think she's better off having a break from me."

"Okay, if you say so."

CHAPTER 28

"Thanks, Mrs. Hopper," Grace said as their last customer stepped out, the front door bell clanging with her departure. As Grace stood in the doorway, Beth Morgan Langdon appeared.

Ruthie's older sister and partner at the farm rarely came into the store. If they needed supplies, Raoul, the livestock manager, usually picked them up, or Ruthie so she could visit with her friend. "Hello," she said, stepping aside to let Beth in.

"No worries, I don't need anything," the tall Morgan daughter said. In jeans and a work jacket, she wore her brown hair tied back in a long braid that reached to her waist. "I asked Lang to pick up the kids so I could stop by to see you."

"Oh? Of course, come in. I'll put the Closed sign up, and we can talk in the office."

As Grace led the way, she wondered what in the world Beth wanted. She barely knew Ruthie's sister, who people called "the quiet Morgan," and she'd had maybe four or five brief conversations with her over the years. When they reached the office, she invited her to sit. "I'll be right back," she said, stepping out to find Paul, encouraging him to go home and assuring him that Beth would walk her home.

Once seated beside her visitor, she said, "How can I help you?"

"I hope this isn't too presumptuous of me, and if it is, I'll leave immediately," Beth said, "but I was hoping that I might help you."

Grace sat up straighter, regarding her. "Oh?"

Beth swallowed hard, then said, "A number of years ago, I went through a very traumatic event. Not the same as yours, but it left me broken, empty, and numb."

Grace began to tremble. "I'm so sorry to hear that. Beth, I'm really grateful to you for thinking of me, but I can't talk about it. I'm trying to move past this and I can't... I mean, I'm not ready."

"That's just it. You can't move anywhere or have any life until you deal with the trauma. You don't know me, but I don't talk to anyone about my feelings, except my husband, sometimes. At other times, I can't even talk to him. I'm like a turtle who pulls her head into her shell and closes the door. No one's gettin' in. You don't have to talk to me about your experience or anything."

"Thank you, because I can't. I'm sorry."

"There's no reason to say a word. I came to see you to say you're not alone. If you ever want to talk, I would be happy to listen. I also wanted to give you this." She handed her a business card. "Haley saved my life. I wouldn't have my husband whom I adore or my two beautiful children if it wasn't for Haley Alvarez. A couple of our family members have worked with Haley, Maggie, for one, Kyle's wife, Harriet and my sister-in-law Rose who's married to our brother Sam. Hayley's office is right here in town."

Grace nodded as she took the card. "People have mentioned her to me."

Beth stood up. "Well, I'll let you get home. I believe this is Scrabble night, is it not?"

"Yes," she answered, "but I can be late."

"Not on my account. My cell number's on the back if you find yourself in a place where you do want to talk."

"Thank you, Beth. I truly am grateful. Can I ask you one thing?"

"Of course."

"Where did you park?"

Beth gave her a quizzical look. "In your lot. Then I walked around to the front."

"Would you mind terribly walking out with me and sitting in your car, watching until I get to the back door of the house?"

"Of course not," Beth replied, her smile warm and reassuring.

As she walked to her house, Grace noticed that the entire time they'd been interacting, the other woman had never tried to touch her. Saying a silent prayer of thanks, she sighed as she opened the back door, turning to wave at Beth as she stepped inside. *She understands.*

SCRABBLE WAS A SMALL GROUP, MOSTLY SENIORS. ARIA WAS MISSING, AS were Tom and Bella. Grace had dreaded seeing him, but her heart clenched with sadness at his absence. As they cleaned up, folding tables and chairs to store in the back room, Brendan passed by her. "Slow night, huh?"

Grace nodded. "Wonder where the others are? Even Chuck and George are out of town."

"Well, I heard Aria went to Portland for a couple of days to visit friends, and by now, Nick and Tom are probably halfway to Faulkner's Ridge ready to kill a couple of touristas."

"Excuse me?"

Brendan laughed. "What a crew. I give a couple of 'em two days and Mr. Foster's helicopter will be deployed."

Grace set down the four chairs she was carrying. "Brendan, what in the world are you talking about?"

"The pack trip. They left early this morning, and there was already enough griping to set Ben Morgan's teeth on edge."

"They went on a pack trip? Who?"

"Couple of TV stars and their entourage. Have you ever seen that Canadian mystery show, *The Veil*?"

"A couple of times."

"Well, the two main stars, Maggie Watkins and Patch Andrews, along with her kids and Patch's airhead girlfriend have probably just made camp in the Painted Valley with Ben, Nick, and Tom doing all the work."

"For how long?" Grace asked, still incredulous at what she was hearing.

"They're out for a week, if they make it. Due back next Wednesday."

As the color drained from her cheeks, she picked her chairs, two under each arm.

"You okay, Grace?"

"Fine," she said, hurrying off. The thought of Tom so far away terrified her. She quickly said her goodbyes and ran out barely holding in her tears till she reached her car.

CHAPTER 29

"Can somebody please give me a break?" Nick asked as the three men pitched tents and prepared for dinner their third night on the trail. "Not only is you-know-who a pain in the neck, but Tara gets spooked every time Raffles gets near her, and she hates to be separated from Raine."

They'd sent the guests to the water to wash up. The mountain stream was still too cold for bathing or swimming, but each person had been given a water bag to do with as they wished. Every night, Ben warned them to fill their bags before they returned to camp, "Because no one's filling them in the middle of the night." He, Tom, and Nick had already filled four water bags each, which they had hidden from the others in case of a water emergency during the night.

Ben laughed. "Sookie's bonded to you, buddy. What can I say?"

"I'll babysit her tomorrow," Tom said, "but you'll have to watch Patch. He practically slides off Raine at every turn. If I could tie a kid's strap around him, I would." Patch and Sookie had been given the ranch's two gentlest mounts, Tara and her sister, Raine, sorrel Morgans. Like sisters, the horses would follow each other to the ends of the earth.

"Gladly. I'll watch out for Patch. Anything to get away from the she-devil."

Later, as they made dinner, the three men discussed the next day's plans. It would be their last easy day before they began the slow ascent to Faulkner's Ridge. They would spend two days on the ridge, then descend and start for home. Before they broke up to tend to various chores, they agreed upon the watch schedule. Tom volunteered for first watch, then Nick and finally Ben from four to sunrise.

They then spent some time considering each rider. The moaning and groaning of the first few nights had subsided, and most were now wearing the right gear. Before they'd left Ben had sent Sookie into town for good jeans, jacket and footwear, which she had initially refused to wear. After freezing in the cool mornings and evening and tearing several of her flimsy shirts and leggings to shreds, she now lived in her jeans and wore several sweaters under her jacket. The rest seemed to have packed sensibly. Early on, they had tasked Ursula and Donnie with watching out for Sonny, her boyfriend. The trio usually rode at the front with Ben. "Ole Sonny's putting on a brave face," he said, "but he's a hurtin' cowboy. Now, if you two will get the cooking finished, I'll give the bathroom talk again while they're having happy hour."

Later, as Tom approached the group to let them know dinner was ready, Ben was completing his lecture. "As always, everyone needs to stay in or very near their tent. And remember, if you have to visit Mother Nature, tell whichever one of us is on watch. Tom'll be up first from nine to one, then Nick till four, then me. Any questions?"

Sookie raised her hand. "What if we prefer to get help from someone who's not on duty?" she asked, batting her thick false eyelashes at Nick.

"Well then, you're out of luck. No exceptions. We need our rest, just like you do," Ben said. "Comprende?"

She hmphed, but said nothing further.

Tom glanced over and noticed Ursula rolling her eyes. There was no love lost between the two Glen offspring and Sookie. So far, Sonny seemed to be trying to keep the peace, but that peace seemed fragile at best. *Poor Sonny*, he thought, watching the shy, affable geologist follow Ursula to the thick calico cloth covered with platters of cold meats, salads and grilled vegetables.

Finally, dinner over and after a short time around the fire, everyone retired to their tents around nine. Flashlight beams were visible as Tom took up watch, but for the most part, peace reigned, punctuated by the distant barks and howls of coyotes. The first night, the coyotes had frightened some of the group, but by now, they were either too tired to care or accustomed to the sounds of the night. "That's the good thing about days on the trail," Ben liked to say. "After a few days of riding, they're too pooped to complain."

Tom settled on a flat boulder that afforded a clear view of the circle of tents. He leaned back, gazing up at the stars and thinking of Grace, of her smooth soft skin and her warm hazel eyes. He had hated to see the terror and anxiety in those beautiful eyes since the attack. What the future would bring, he was uncertain, but he knew in some way, she had to be in it. As he sat enjoying the relatively warm night, scuffling to his left broke the silence.

"Get away from me, you little rat!" More scuffling. It sounded like Ursula's voice.

As Tom got up to investigate, wafts of marijuana reached his nose. "Geez, what now?" he said, calling out, "Ursula, is that you?"

"Aaahh! Eeeee!" came from the brush, followed by a much stronger smell. As he watched, Ursula crashed through to the fire area, and a small black-and-white creature scuttered off to her left.

Frantically, Ursula pulled off her boots, then her jeans and threw them on the ground, stamping them into the dirt.

"What the hell?" Ben asked as he and Nick came over. Sonny emerged from the brush shortly after his girlfriend, but he appeared unscathed.

Tom looked over at his fellow guides. "Hog-nosed skunk. Cute little fella. Direct hit."

"Fuck you!" Ursula cried, hands on hips, now standing by the fire in her underwear. "Do something!"

Milly and Buddy stood outside their tent now, both in sweats. She shook her head. "Serves you right, out smoking your pot when you're supposed to be getting a good night's sleep."

"How do you think I get a good night's sleep, Mother? If it weren't for the pot, I wouldn't sleep at all, or I'd be on Ambien or some other shit like you."

Buddy took a few steps toward his daughter, but not too close. "Don't talk to your mom like that, Ursie."

"Then tell her to shut the hell up! Now what am I going to do?"

Ben stepped forward, exchanging looks with Tom and Nick. "For one thing, you're going to shut up yourself. Because of your stupidity and breaking the rules, we're all up and are going to have to deal with this noxious odor now and on the trail." He grabbed a backpack from their supplies, from which he extracted a white plastic spray bottle of Skunk Away.

"Do you know that in all the pack trips I've been on, I've never once had to use this? Now, where did it hit you?"

Dumbfounded, and also slightly stoned, Ursula indicated her left leg from hip to foot, which he saturated with the spray. "You've got more jeans, right?" he asked, regarding the liquid cascading down her anorexically thin legs. Ursula nodded, and he sent Sonny into their tent to get jeans, underwear and socks. "Grab a clean shirt too," Ben called as Sonny disappeared.

"Talk about skeleton woman," Sookie said, a trifle too loudly. She and Patch had also arisen and were observing.

"That's not helping hon," Patch said.

"Damn right, it isn't. You shut up too," Ben said to Sookie, then turned to Nick. "Grab one of the water buckets and throw in the hydrogen peroxide, a scoop of baking soda, and dish soap. We'll soak 'em overnight and air dry 'em on the ride tomorrow."

"Hydrogen peroxide! Oh no you don't! Those are my favorite jeans!"

Ignoring her protest, Ben said, "You go around the back of your tent, take your underwear off and throw it to Nick."

Sonny emerged with the clean clothes, and after Ursula tossed him the soiled ones, he handed them to her. Tom noticed that he kept himself at arm's length and returned to the fire as quickly as possible.

"Okay, folks, show's over. Time to get some sleep," Ben said. Nick began soaking the clothes as the others retreated to their tents.

"What about me?" Ursula whined as she came from behind the tent. "I still reek."

"Here, grab a sponge and you can wash with the mixture Nick just made in the bucket. It'll probably help. Smell should fade in a couple of days."

"A couple of days!"

"Maybe by tomorrow night. We'll have to see, won't we? Nothing more we can do tonight. Sonny, your choice, man. You can bunk with Ursula or sleep under the stars with Nick and me."

Donnie poked his head out. "He can share my tent. No one should have to sleep with that stink."

"I repeat—what about me? How am I supposed to sleep?"

Ben observed her for thirty seconds, then said, "I'd suggest that Sonny remove everything except your sleeping bag and stow it all in your brother's tent for tonight. That way, the stink will be contained. We'll deal with cleaning your tent tomorrow, if needed. Now, try to sleep as best you can. You're welcome to bed out here by the fire, if you'd rather? Air you out a little."

"Assholes," she muttered, stomping over to her tent and zippering herself in without another word, even to Sonny, who had cleared their belongings out in record time.

Tom and the others straightened things up, left the clothes in the bucket, and stoked the fire. "I'll finish up," Tom said. "You two get some sleep."

"Yeah, right," Ben said. "With that stink?"

CHAPTER 30

The door to an inner office opened, and a short round, barefooted woman in black yoga pants and a purple tunic sweater appeared. Her curly silver hair flowed over her shoulders to her waist. "You must be Grace? I'm Haley. Welcome. Please come in." She stepped aside and ushered Grace into a light, plant-filled space with a sofa and two overstuffed armchairs. "Would you like something to drink? Tea? Water?"

"I'd love some tea, if it's easy?"

"Please make yourself comfortable," she said, waving to one of the armchairs. The therapist grabbed a basket of assorted varieties of tea bags, and Grace chose a lavender chai and popped it into the mug Haley held in her other hand. "Anything in it? Honey or sweetener?"

"Nothing, thanks."

The kettle boiled instantly. After pouring two teas, Haley set one on the table beside Grace. She then curled up in the opposite chair, teacup in hand and tucked legs beneath her, straightening her sweater. "So, how can I help?"

Grace's hand shook as she picked up her mug. "To be honest, I'm not sure."

"Are you troubled?"

Grace nodded. "Troubled, scared, anxious, numb, a complete

mess. It's like my insides have been ripped out and there's nothing left inside."

"You are still in there somewhere, of this I'm certain," Hayley said. "Describing what brought you to this state might be useful? Would you like to tell me a little about yourself?"

Grace swallowed. "I work with my dad at Valley Hardware. Now that I've met you, I've seen you in the store. Somehow, you look different."

Haley smiled. "In a store, I'm in my shopping clothes. These," she added, sweeping her arms in front of her, "are my work clothes."

Grace returned her smile. "They're lovely, and they look very comfortable."

"Thank you. Please go on, when you're ready."

"The attack happened at the store, late in the evening. While it stopped short of rape, that was the man's intention. My father intervened just as... It happened a few weeks ago. My bruises have mostly healed, but the rest of me hasn't.

"I'd met a man a short time before and we... It happened fast... We grew close almost immediately, and it had the beginnings of a precious, loving relationship. He was...is the kindest, most caring person I've ever met."

"How wonderful for both of you."

"It's gone. I destroyed it. Since the attack, I can't bear to be touched. I've driven him away in the cruelest way."

"I should think if he cares about you, he'd understand."

"He does. It's me. I can't have him near me. When someone, anyone, touches me, I feel nauseous and sick."

"That's very normal under the circumstances."

"But how can I change this, or can I change it?"

"Only you can answer that, Grace. You and I can work together. I would love to help and support you. There are many ways to work through trauma, but the revulsion you have to touch might also best be treated by a trauma specialist. I know a wonderful person in Tucson. Would you be interested in seeing her?"

Grace nodded. "Where do we go? You and I?"

"Why don't you tell me as much as you're comfortable with about yourself, growing up, whatever seems important, and we'll go from there."

An hour later, the two women rose and said goodbye. As they said goodbyes, Grace felt the beginnings of peace in her heart, a peace she had imagined was lost forever.

Haley held out her hands. "No need to go further. Just want you to know that my arms are always here."

Grace took her hands and held on for several seconds. "Thank you."

THERE WAS STILL AN ODOR OF SKUNK IN THE BREEZE AS THE GROUP started out the next morning, but it was bearable. By popular vote, and because she was a decent rider, Ursula was consigned to bring up the rear. Tom rode just ahead, keeping an eye on her. Sookie was now in front of him, complaining about a million things at once—missing Nickie, the godawful smell, saddle sores, the heat, the cold, almost anything that came to mind. Impervious to her whining, Tom kept his attention on the trail and the rider behind him. By midday, Ben had led them to the base of the ridge, where he decided they would stop for lunch.

"Fill up your canteens and water bags now, because there's no reliable water source once we get on the ridge," he told the assembled group. "We'll have lunch ready in a few minutes."

"What about those old nags you're dragging along with us? Can't they haul extra water?" Sookie asked.

"The pack horses can only carry so much," Ben said. "Your choice, but water will be rationed up there, so the more we take of our own, the better off we'll be." Sookie harrumphed as she strode off, carrying her two designer water bottles and the water bag she'd been issued.

After the lunch things were packed and everyone was ready, Ben called them all together. "Listen carefully, folks. We're about to tackle one of the two most difficult legs of the trip. The trail gets very narrow, and there are a lot of falling rocks. The horses know what they're doing, but you still have to be vigilant every minute. Even experienced riders can get hurt climbing and descending the ridge. So, go slow, listen to your guide, and keep a firm hold on your horse. Questions?"

Sookie raised her hand. "Okay, you're freaking me out, Bennie. Can't I walk up and have someone else take my horse?"

"No. That's dangerous for you and your horse. Other questions?"

"How long's the climb?" Buddy asked.

"Couple of hours, maybe three," Ben said.

"I don't want my daughter at the rear. I'll take it."

Ben considered that a minute, then said, "You can ride behind her, then Sookie and Tom. He's got to be at the back to bring the pack horses along."

After a heated discussion where Ben refused to yield, they mounted and made their way to the trailhead punctuated by numerous switchbacks and narrow, crumbling sections. Tom started to wonder whether he'd make it, never mind Sookie and her boyfriend, who rode just in front of Nick. Sonny proved to be a careful, studious pupil, and his riding had greatly improved during the trip, especially the past two days. Watching him five riders ahead, Tom said a silent prayer of thanks. *One less person with the potential to fall off the cliff.*

Three hours later, they could see the ridge ahead, and the first few riders had reached level ground. As Sonny and Cocoa climbed onto the ridge, Donnie on the tall Friesian, Raffles, right behind him, Tom heard popping and squealing in the bushes left of the trail and a squadron of six javelinas crossed in front of Patch and Raine. The horse whinnied and backed up, but remained calm as the medium-sized pig-like peccaries with their coarse fur and strong odor flew by into the brush on the other side.

Close call, Tom thought, as javelinas could be quite aggressive at times and had been known to attack horses and riders.

Up ahead, Patch called, "What the hell are those?" He swayed to one side to get a better look.

"Watch what you're doing!" Nick cried.

Too late. Patch slipped from his saddle and landed on a pile of rocks.

Before Tom could act, Buddy hopped from his horse, handed the reins to Ursula, and climbed up to where his wife's costar was splayed on the ground moaning and groaning.

Unable to leave Sookie, Tom called, "Buddy, that's too dangerous! Go back to your horse and let us handle it!"

Buddy ignored him and was attempting to help Patch to sit when Ben and Nick, who had already reached the level ground and secured their horses, joined them. "We'll take it from here," Ben said, shoving Buddy out of the way as Nick lifted Patch. "Get back to your horse. Now."

The stocky rancher looked like he wanted to argue, but then turned, scurried back down the trail, and with some difficulty remounted Royal.

"His arm's broken," Nick said as they helped Patch to his feet.

"Okay," Ben said, "You walk him up, and I'll ride Raine." He turned to the rest of them waiting down trail. "All set, folks. Take it nice and easy. The javelinas are gone, but this section is rocky. Everyone ready?"

"No! I am not ready!" Sookie cried. "I can't make it."

"Yes, you can," Tom said behind her. "Tara'll get you there. Just hold her tight. I'm right behind you."

"Can't I ride with you?" she whimpered.

Ben leapt up onto Raine, calling over his shoulder. "No, you can't. Now, buck up, Ms. Shaw! You've got people and horses depending on you."

The line began moving, Nick and Patch walking at the rear behind the pack horses. Sookie sniffled, but obediently urged Tara forward. "Okay, girl. We can do this."

Good girl, Tom thought, wondering for the millionth time why the hell they'd allowed her to come on the trip.

CHAPTER 31

Early Friday afternoon, Grace walked out of her second appointment with Marie de Leon feeling as if a weight was slowly lifting from her chest. Marie's touch, light the first visit, felt more like a massage this time. Initially, the therapist's touch had felt like burning coals or made her skin prickle, icy cold, but slowly, Grace was becoming more comfortable with the sensations. The trauma therapist had an office in the Catalina foothills west of Tucson, which she shared with an acupuncturist and two other massage therapists. Her treatment room was like a warm cocoon, and Grace had felt surprisingly safe from the moment she entered.

At Marie's suggestion, she had booked two sessions for the following week and also a massage with one of the other women therapists. All the driving back and forth to Tucson as well as another session with Haley meant that she'd spent little time at the store and no time at Valley Stables with Dusty. She missed the strong, steady creature and his gentle snuffing as she petted him, but she also felt guilty at the way she'd run out on him the week before. "I want to be healed before I see him again," she told Haley.

Haley had asked if seeing Dusty might actually be healing for her, to which she had no response. *One step at a time*, she thought, slipping into the car for the drive home. She checked her cell phone continually, but there were no calls from Tom. Both relieved and sad, she resolved to put her energies into getting well. *Just like Dusty. Let me heal before I hurt Tom any more than I already have.*

She found her father chatting with a customer when she returned. Nodding to Paul, who was behind the register, she headed back to the office to get checks cut for Paulo and Paul. A few minutes later, Wilbur poked his head in. "How was your appointment, honey?"

"Good… Helpful, I think."

"Whaddya think? Takeout tonight, or you want to head over to your aunt's?"

"I vote Gracie's. Be good to see Auntie."

Ben worked on Patch's arm as Tom and Nick made camp. Patch then retreated to their tent with a heavy dose of painkillers, and the rest of the party scattered around, chatting, taking photos of the incredible sunset, or washing up. Later, as they prepared dinner, the three guides huddled out of earshot of the others.

Ben shook his head. "The last five trips, there hasn't been a single glitch, so I guess we were due. First skunks and now this. I'm no doc, but I've set it. It's his right arm, guys. No way he can ride. We're gonna have to get him out of here somehow."

"What's the plan, boss?" Nick asked as he stoked the fire.

"If you two can handle this," he said, waving at the dinner offerings they'd unpacked. "I'm gonna roam around and see if I can get cell service. No signal here, but we're in a depression. If I climb up a bit, I may be able to get the ranch. I'm thinking Spark's helicopter if it's free."

"Is there enough space to land?" Tom asked, gazing around at the bowl-shaped clearing ringed with rocks and boulders.

"There's a place about a mile along the ridge. It's wide enough for a landing. Patch will just have to walk it."

As Ben set off, Nick looked up at Tom. "Here we go. What next?"

~

"WHAT'S HAPPENED?" LEONORA ASKED, NOTICING HER HUSBAND'S FACE as he hung up the phone.

"Been an injury on Faulkner's Ridge."

"Oh no! I told Ben that group wasn't up to it. That trail is in terrible shape! Who's hurt?"

"That Patch fella. One of the beginner riders. Javelinas startled him, and he fell off his horse and broke his arm."

"Land sakes! I'm surprised the javelinas were up that high this time of year."

"I've gotta call Spark. Ben says the fella can't ride. Wondering about the helicopter."

"Spark's out of town. Left for Portland this morning," she said. Portland was the headquarters for Foster Enterprises. Spark had sold his Portland home, but still kept a condo there for his twice-monthly visits.

"Lemme check anyway. Mickey's probably with him," Ben said, referring to Spark's pilot, "but that other fella, Archie McKee, can fly the helo if it's here."

A few minutes later, Ben reported that the helicopter was indeed at Grenville Airport in a hangar Spark had purchased. "Spark got a hold of McKee, and he's headed up here now. He'll pick me up at the camp, and we'll head out." He referred to Emma's Dream, the ranch's summer camp for handicapped children started by his son Ben and Maggie. It had the largest open space on the ranch.

Leonora paced back and forth. "Oh no you don't! I forbid you to go up in that thing. Mickey is one thing, but I don't know this Archie. It's windy today and—"

"Now, Nora," he said, putting his arms around her. "I'll be fine."

"Why can't Robbie go? Or Lang? Anyone but you?"

He kissed the top of her head. "Because it's my job. Now, I've gotta call Ben. He's waiting on high ground to hear from me."

~

Ben returned to the campsite and gathered everyone to explain what would happen in the morning. "If Patch is going, I'm going," Sookie announced, arms folded tight over her chest.

"That may not be possible weight wise, so don't get your hopes up. It's a small helicopter. If it's just the pilot, you might fit, but if they brought an extra person to help navigate, it can only take Patch.

Doped up and white as a sheet, Patch said little and returned to his tent after eating a few bites of dinner. The three guides watched Sookie help him into the tent. "Finally making herself useful," Nick muttered as they cleaned and stowed the dinner things.

Ben shook his head. "It's a bad break. I pray it doesn't get infected before we get him out of here." He gazed around. "We're going have to hang the food bags with javelinas nearby. They're a pain in the ass to chase away if they smell food. Don't have a lot of choice, but those two scraggly bristlecone pines will have to do. I'll grab the ropes."

Despite their efforts, the javelina squadron invaded shortly after midnight on Tom's watch, causing a ruckus as they rooted around for food. Unsurprisingly to anyone, Sookie had ignored instructions and stowed granola bars and candy in the tent. Her screams brought Tom running just in time to see the tent collapse, poor Patch trapped inside as she flailed and fought a losing battle to save her stash.

"Throw the food out before you get hurt," Tom yelled as he grabbed several pots and began banging them together. While the others ran off, a large male javelina stood his ground at the door of the tent. He looked really to gobble anything in sight, including Sookie's feet as she kicked out at him.

"Geez," Ben said as he and Nick joined them, Buddy right behind. Each held fistfuls of rocks. The remaining animals had retreated to the bushes, but the male smelled food and refused to budge.

"He's gonna bite her," Tom said. "These high-ground javelina are nasty."

"All javelina are nasty," Nick said." Where's the Skunk Away? That might scare him off."

Ben retrieved the bottle from one of hanging backpacks. Unfazed by the loud banging all around him, the javelina took a step into the collapsed tent.

"Shoot it," Buddy said as he continued to pepper the animal with rocks. "You brought guns, didn't you?"

"Good plan with two people inside," Nick muttered as Ben rushed up with the Skunk Away and pushed by the others.

Getting as close as he could, he aimed for the animal's eyes just as the javelina clamped down on Sookie's ankle. "Eee!" she cried out.

The acidic spray did the trick, and the animal released her, stepped back, and ran to join the others. Sookie's ankle dripped blood as Tom untangled her from the tent and carried her toward the fire. Gently, he set her down and wrapped a towel around her ankle. "I'll be right back soon as we get Patch out."

A few minutes later, Patch sat beside her as Nick fixed the tent and Ben ran for the first aid kit. "This is a nightmare," he muttered to Tom in a low voice. "Javelina carry rabies. It's rare, but they do. She'll have to be treated."

Tom knelt in front of Sookie, who was alternating between sobbing and shouting obscenities. He couldn't tell whether she was in pain, frightened, or angry. Probably all three, he mused as he unwrapped the towel and wiped the blood away in order to examine the bite marks ringing her ankle.

"Not too deep. They'll heal up okay," he said, smiling at her.

"Don't try to cheer me up! I'm hurting, poor Patch is a mess, and I'm getting off this mountain tomorrow if I have to fly the helicopter myself!"

A short time later, Sookie's wound cleaned and dressed, they loaded her up with painkillers and Tom helped her back to the tent. He promised that whoever was on watch would stay right outside their tent. After she and Patch were settled, Tom scoured the space for food, confiscating the box of granola bars and bag of candy, which he tied into a bag and hung beside the others in the tree.

"You okay to keep watch for another hour?" Ben asked him.

"Yup. Hope you two can get some rest."

Ben shook his head. "I forgot to ask Dad if anyone'd be coming with the pilot, but if they do, they better know how to ride, 'cause she has to go back with Patch and get a rabies shot pronto."

"Night," Tom said as the two others headed for their bedrolls.

CHAPTER 32

"Hey, Ruthie," Grace said as her friend came into the store Monday morning. "Careful you don't trip over those seed bags. The guys haven't had a chance to move them."

"I'm just grabbing our shipment of early spinach seeds. Your dad ordered them for us. Are they here?"

"Out back," Grace said, "but they're fifty-pound bags. I'll get Paul to load them in the truck." She disappeared, returning a few minutes later to find her friend sitting on a stool at the side of the counter.

"You okay? You look uncomfortable."

Ruthie gave her a weak smile, sweat glistening on her round, pretty face. "My ankles are swollen, my feet hurt, I look like a beached whale, and I'm almost useless out at the farm."

"Then maybe you should take time off? Want me to call someone to come get you? Harley?"

"He's in Sonoita looking at some horses. Again."

"How about your mom or dad? Paul or Paulo can drive your truck, and we'll pick him up."

"Dad's gone up in Spark's helicopter. Someone's hurt up on Faulkner's Ridge. Thank God Harley didn't go. Last few trips have gone off without a hitch, but not this one, apparently. My husband has a very short temper, just like my oldest brother."

Impatiently, Grace listened until Ruthie paused. "Who's hurt?" *Please let it not be Tom!*

"Some guy fell off his horse and broke his arm. One of the guests, I'm pretty sure."

Grace let go of the breath she'd been holding. "But everyone else is okay?"

"Far as I know," Ruthie said, reaching over to pat her arm. "He'll be fine, dearie. Tom's one of the best riders I've ever seen. He's levelheaded and steady. Try not to worry."

Before she could stop them, tears snaked down Grace's cheeks. She turned away, reaching for a tissue, but not before her friend spied her distress.

"Hey, hey, this is typical pack trip stuff. Everyone's fine. They're just bringing the guy back 'cause he can't ride. It'd be dangerous coming down the ridge with a broken right arm."

Grace shook her head. "It's not that. It's just... I've made such a mess of things. I have no right to say anything about Tom. I pushed him away, and he probably hates me."

"Now, you know that's not true." Ruthie heaved herself up to standing. "I gotta get moving. Do you think the bags are loaded?"

"All set," Grace said after checking the parking lot. "Are you sure you don't want one of us to drive you?"

"No, but thanks. I just like to complain. I'm fine, really. Maybe I'll drop the seeds off and go home and take a nap. The crew can start the planting without me, and I can ask Mom to pick up Charlotte from the Cottage."

The women hugged, then Ruthie climbed slowly up into the truck. "Hang in there," she said, smiling at Grace. "I'll let you know if I hear anything."

"Thanks, take care." Grace watched as her friend backed out of the lot. *Thank goodness I see Hayley in an hour, then down to Tucson for Marie,* she thought, heading back inside. *I sure need them today!*

THE MILE-LONG JOURNEY ALONG THE RIDGE PROCEEDED WITHOUT incident. Ben led the group with Ursula and Sonny right behind him. Donnie followed, leading Tara, and then his parents, with Buddy leading Raine. Nick took charge of the three pack horses, and they followed him and Raffles. Finally, Sookie rode with Tom on Echo just behind Patch, who was walking. Tom suspected that Sookie was perfectly capable of walking as well, but she'd put up such a fuss at breakfast that they acquiesced and allowed her to ride with him on the flat, relatively wide ridge trail.

When they arrived at the designated landing spot, they tethered the horses farther down the trail, well away from where the helicopter would touch down. Ben instructed everyone to find a comfortable spot at the edge of the clearing and grab a snack. They hadn't long to wait before *thwip, thwap, thwop* and chuffing sounds alerted them to the helicopter's approach. Suddenly, like a phoenix, it rose from below, first at eye level, then higher. Archie circled, determining the best angle for his approach.

Ben looked and his heart sank as he saw who sat next to the pilot. "Shit, my mother will skin me alive."

Tom gazed over at him, wondering at his words. He looked back at the craft as it hovered, then came to the ground, blades chuffing to a stop. His boss, Ben Morgan Senior, sat in the copilot seat. An expert rider, he hadn't been on the trail in years and only took the occasional pleasure ride with his buddy Spark. "Uh-oh," he said, waving as the two men alit.

"Hey, Dad," Ben said, hugging the tall, handsome man wearing a leather jacket, Stetson, and a black backpack slung over his shoulder. "We've got a problem."

His father grinned. "That's why I brought this, just in case."

"What's in there?"

"My meds and whatever I need for a few days on the trail. We didn't know what we were gonna find up here, did we, Archie?"

The short, dark-haired pilot nodded, sliding his earphones down around his neck. "This thing will only hold three. Spark's larger helo is in the shop for repairs."

"Dad, this is a very bad idea."

Ben Senior grasped his son's shoulder. "Only one you got, buddy. Now, who needs a ride home?"

Ben filled Archie in on Patch's condition and then explained about Sookie. "They both have to go to Valley Hospital, but she's the most critical. Think you can land this in Grenville and have a car or ambulance there to transport them?"

"No problem. I'll call over there as soon as we're in the air. One of Spark's cars is always there, usually a limo."

They loaded the two passengers in with little fuss or drama from Sookie. After a brief conversation, the helicopter started up with a *throp, thrip, thrap* and rose into the air. They spied Sookie waving from the rear window, a huge grin on her face as the helo turned and chuffed off out of sight. "No worries, folks. Archie'll get them safely to the hospital in no time. Now, how're we doing?" Ben asked, gazing around at the group.

Ursula rolled her eyes. "How does total disaster of a trip sound?"

Her mother waved her hand. "Don't mind her. It's been lovely so far. My daughter's pouting because of the skunk episode, but the rest of us, who know how to follow rules, are fine."

Buddy nodded, turning to Ben Senior. "Ditto what Milly said. I've been having a grand ole time on Royal here, but I understand he's your horse?"

"That he is and a good ole fella to boot."

"I think you should ride him going forward. I'm happy on one of the Morgans."

"You sure?" Ben Senior said. "This is your trip after all."

"And that is your horse. I'll take whichever one the guys tell me to."

Young Ben looked at the two men, then said, "Thanks, Buddy. That's kind of you. Why don't you start with Raine? Tara will follow her to the end of the earth, so they should do just fine."

"Raine it is," Buddy said, winking at Ben Senior.

They decided to have an early lunch before pushing on. As they packed up to go, Ben Senior asked Tom, "You think this gang'll make it to Connor Pass, where we start down?"

Tom grinned. "At this point, I hate to risk jinxing us by saying yes. With the exception of Sonny, the rest are competent, experienced riders, so that's a plus."

His boss chuckled. "That's what we like to hear—pluses! Come on, ole boy," he said, patting Royal before mounting the tall, strong Morgan in one fluid motion.

Tom shook his head. *Like a twenty-year-old*, he mused, watching as man and horse melded into one as they headed down the trail.

"OH MY GOD, OH MY GOD!" LEONORA SAID, PACING BACK AND FORTH IN her daughter-in-law's kitchen. "What was your husband thinking letting this happen?"

Maggie watched her as the kids played with their cousins Lily and Charlotte in the backyard. Beth was nursing three-month-old Parker while trying in vain to calm her mother down. "Dad's a strong, healthy man and an expert horseman. He'll be fine."

"What about his heart?" her mother cried. "He hasn't ridden more than a few miles in years, and he has none of his pills or, oh my goodness, I need to phone Chester."

"Archie phoned. Ben said big Ben brought all his meds with him."

"I knew it! I knew it! That big stupid lug of a man knew he'd be joining the trip! I'm going to kill him *and* his son when they get back!"

A few minutes later, Ruthie waddled in, accompanied by Grace. "Hey, all," she said. "Harley's not back so I asked Grace to drive me over here."

Beth's eyes narrowed as she stared at her sister. "Why? Are you feeling worse?"

Ruthie waved her hand dismissively. "No, but if I don't have to drive, I don't. Any word from Ben?"

Maggie shook her head. "Archie should have the two injured riders to the hospital by now so that's a relief."

"Where's Dad? Did he leave a car in Grenville? I can have Harley swing over and pick him up if needed."

"Your father is on Faulkner's Ridge with your brother. He's joined the trip."

"Why?" Ruthie asked, her blue eyes widening.

"Because he couldn't fit in the helicopter."

Her daughter plopped down on a kitchen chair. "Yikes."

"I'm going to call and demand that Archie go back and pick him up! That's what I'll do," Leonora said.

"They're probably five or six hours from the landing spot, and Ben says there's nowhere else safe to land."

"That's ridiculous."

"That's Faulkner's Ridge, Mom," Ruthie said. "Dad'll be fine. I'm sure he's in cowboy heaven riding with Ben and that Buddy. They'll be gabbing from dawn till dusk."

"Why don't you sit, Leonora," Maggie said. "I'll make us all some tea."

Grace gazed around at the group of Morgan women and thought again how lucky they were to have each other. As Maggie laid the tea things out, moving slowly around the kitchen, she said, "Why don't you let me do that, Maggie."

CHAPTER 33

"Look at him," Ben said to Tom as they rode side by side. "Like a pig in shit."

His father had insisted he lead the way after lunch, telling them, "I know these mountains like the back of my hand."

"Back of my hand, my eye," his son muttered. "He's just happy to be free. I bet it's fifteen years or more since he's been out here."

Tom grinned, observing his boss. "You'd never know it. He and Royal are bonded, aren't they?"

Ben nodded. "Was a relief that Buddy offered to switch horses. Dad never would have asked, but I was about to. Royal will take good care of him."

That evening, as Nick and Tom put up the tents, Ben and his dad made the fire and cooked dinner—hamburgers and hot dogs from the dry ice bags, along with beans and Carmela's homemade brown bread. "It'll be good to get down by the river tomorrow. Maybe we can catch some trout for dinner," Ben said.

His father looked up from the fire. "I know your mama's about to bust a gourd, but I have to admit, this is fun. Like old times. Maybe when her hips are completely healed, I can drag her up here again. Nothin' like it."

His son shook his head. "Good luck with that."

"Wait'll I tell her all about it."

"Easy for you to say. You're not the one she's gonna rips to shreds when we get home."

"You worry too much son. I'll smooth things over lickety-split."

"Yeah, right," Ben said, tossing a stick into the fire.

Ben Senior took Sookie and Patch's tent. The guides stacked both the guest mats and sleeping bags on top of one another to, his son said, "make things extra soft for the ole cowboy." The old cowboy retired shortly after supper to "the tent of doom," as Nick now called it. They made sure to give the tent a thorough sweep and shake out in case there were still crumbs or bits of contraband food lying around.

The following day, shortly after lunch, they had "one more photo shoot" before preparing to descend from the ridge and into the westernmost part of Painted Valley. The views from this part of the mountain were spectacular, stretching for hundreds of miles in every direction. "This is the why of this trip," Ben said to the others as cameras and cell phones snapped away. "Why we take this route and climb this ridge instead of another. Cool, huh?"

"Beautiful," Milly said, asking Tom to take some family photos, first of her and Buddy, then all the kids, including Sonny. For all her star status, the family matriarch had proven to be a quiet, responsible member of the party. A capable, strong horsewoman, she handled Whimsy with care and ease. The chocolate Morgan belonged to Jaybo Dillon, Lang's father and a dear friend of the elder Morgans. Martha and Jaybo Dillon owned Saguaro Winery, just south of the ranch. Since Jaybo was not well and hadn't been for years, they'd sent both Whimsy and Martha's pinto, Dandy, to live at the Morgan's Run stables, where they were loved and cared for. Both horses were used for lessons and trail riding.

Finally, Ben called, "Time to head down, folks. Snap a couple more shots, then head to your horses." He then went to find his dad.

Ben Senior raised one hand. "I know! I know what you're gonna say. I'm happy to follow your lead. Where do you want me?"

"Tom's taking the rear with Sonny, then Ursula in front of him. Nick's riding in front of Ursula, then the rest of the family. I was going to suggest Donnie, then Buddy with Milly after her son. You choose, Dad. You can ride just behind me or before or after Nick."

His father grinned, blue eyes twinkling. "When do I ever get to ride with my son? I'll go second, if you're okay with it?"

"Fine. Are you okay after a night on the ground?"

Ben had watched his father's every move since he'd emerged from the tent in the morning. Aside from a little stiffness, he seemed fine.

"Fit as a fiddle and raring to go."

"Good. This is the worst section. For the next hour, there'll be falling rocks, narrow paths, and washouts. You heard my lecture to everyone at lunch. Be careful and take it really slow. Donnie'll take his cues from you, so please, Dad, don't rush it."

"I'll be fine, son. I'll be careful, and I've got the greatest guide in the world right ahead of me."

"Yeah, right. Let's hope so," his son said, patting Royal before whistling for Rowdy.

～

THE DESCENT TOOK SEVERAL HOURS. THERE WERE A FEW HAIRY moments where Sonny's horse, Cocoa, slipped on the narrow path, but the gentle gray quarter horse, a favorite with children who took lessons at the ranch, never panicked. He paused, gazed around, then stepped carefully forward with little direction from his rider. Fortunately, Sonny remained calm as well.

They reached their campsite in an open spot by the Gila River a little after four, and Tom, Nick, and Ben broke out the fishing gear, inviting anyone who wanted to throw in a line to grab a reel. Buddy and his son expressed interest, so they accompanied Nick and Ben Senior down to the river. Ben and the others watered the horses, and Sonny helped Tom pitch the tents.

"How're you doing, man?" Tom asked Sonny.

"Fine now. Not sure I've ever been so scared in my life."

Tom smiled. "You'd never know from where I was sitting. You handled yourself really well."

"Cocoa, you mean."

"Horses sense fear. You were calm, so she stayed calm. You did great."

Sonny shrugged, but couldn't quite hide his huge shit-eating grin.

"Tom's right. You've come a long way in a short time," Ben said.

"Gotta keep up with all you expert riders."

Ben nodded. "Actually, it's easier when you're around people who know what they're doing on a horse. I'm sorry their trip got cut short, but without Sookie and Patch, everybody's calmer. Tom's right, horses sense fear."

The expedition to the river was very successful, and the fishermen returned with a long string of trout. Sated and relaxed after a dinner that included wine and enough trout to feed an army, everyone retired happy, the swooshing sounds of the river lulling them to sleep.

Ben was on watch in the early morning, when a cry of "Ouch!" came from Ursula and Sonny's tent.

"Get my boot," Ursula cried. "Smash it."

"Oh geez," Ben said as Tom woke and came running.

The couple crashed out of the tent, Ursula half dressed, Sonny writhing in pain, his wrist already swollen. "A scorpion," she said. "I killed it, but it gave him a good sting."

Once again, Ben went for the first aid kit, then stopped to examine the squished creature in the tent. He then washed Sonny's arm with soap and water and applied a cold emergency ice pack. "How's it feel, buddy?"

Clearly in a lot of pain, Sonny winced. "Burning and tingly. Geez, it hurts."

"That should decrease in the next few hours. We'll keep the ice on it, twenty minutes on, ten off, and keep repeating. We have more packs. It may start itching, but I'd rather not give you Benadryl if we can help it. We'll start with Tylenol and see how you do with that. Sound good?"

Sonny nodded as Ben stood and joined Tom and Nick. His dad was chatting with Buddy and Milly, reassuring them. "Talk about a cursed trip. In all the time I've been leading these things, no one, I mean no one, has ever been bitten by a scorpion. We can't get home soon enough!"

"Anything else we can do for him?" Tom asked.

"Let's see how he is in an hour. Maybe the person on watch should check him every hour throughout the night. If he's gonna have a major allergic reaction, it'll probably be soon, but I'd rather not take any chances."

"Think he can make it back, boss?" Nick asked.

Ben shrugged. "Guess he'll have to. Only option would be to get an ATV out here tomorrow. Let's see how he does tonight."

CHAPTER 34

Thoughts of Tom never left her mind as Grace went through the week, with two appointments with Marie and one with Hayley on Wednesday morning for a "progress check."

As she sat in the therapist's waiting room, she wondered if she had, indeed, made progress.

Later, when Hayley asked the question, she said, "It's one thing for Marie or the masseuse to touch me. That seems therapeutic, but Tom would be different."

"Some would say his touch might be more comforting. He's not your attacker, but a man who has demonstrated a deep caring for you."

"Yes, you're right. I guess I'll have to wait and see."

"Are they back?" Hayley asked.

She shook her head. "Not till tomorrow. The injured riders delayed their progress a bit. Ruthie has been keeping me posted."

They talked awhile longer, then said goodbye. Grace strolled down Main Street, enjoying the peace and calm she always experienced after talking with Hayley. Her thoughts were interrupted by a voice calling from across the street. "Hi, Grace!"

She looked up to find Bella crossing the quiet street. "Hi, how are you?" she said.

Bella smiled her beautiful warm smile. "Great. Just had a fabulous lunch at your aunt's."

"She is a good cook," Grace said.

"I've got a patient, so I have to run," Bella said. "Will I see you at Scrabble?"

"Yes, of course. Have you heard anything from your brother?"

"Not a peep, but I didn't expect to. His cell phone is on his dresser at home. My next patient is Maggie Morgan. If I hear anything, I'll tell you tonight. Take care," Bella said, hurrying off.

Please God make everything be okay, Grace said, heading back to the store.

~

"You and the baby are doing just fine," Bella said, helping Maggie to sit after her examination.

"Are the contractions just Braxton-Hicks, do you think?"

Bella nodded. "You're not dilated at all, so yes, I'd say what you're experiencing are indeed Braxton-Hicks."

"It's just they're so strong," Maggie said, her eyes rimmed with tears. "And with Ben away, I think I'm extra nervous."

"Of course you are," Bella said, placing her hand over Maggie's. "Anxiety and worry make you tense, so that might intensify the pain a bit. Have you ever taken a mindfulness class or meditation workshop?"

Maggie shook her head. "When would I have time between the kids and the stables?"

Bella smiled. "Running after young kids may be another factor. Your Emma's a sweetie, and I'm sure she's a big help."

"She is, but the other one!"

"He's busy, isn't he? Have you had any help this week with Ben away?"

"My in-laws are great, and they pick up the kids from the Cottage almost every day and keep them till the end of my work day. My dad helps too, but Ben's a handful for him. At least at the

Big House, there are three of them...or now two, Leonora and Carmela."

"They're due back tomorrow, I hear. Think you can hang on till then?"

Maggie laughed. "Do I have a choice? Robbie and Hope are bringing dinner tonight, and they're both great with the kids. It'll be fine."

"How are things out in the wilderness? Have you heard from your husband?"

"No, but that's not unusual. Cell service is really spotty. He sent a short text before they headed down from the ridge, but nothing since then."

"I hope your father-in-law's holding up okay."

"Me too. Leonora's ready to skin my Ben alive. I suspect this is the most fun big Ben's had in a long time. He loves riding and being out there."

"Well, you take care. You have my number. If you need anything, don't hesitate to call."

At the end of the evening as players packed up Scrabble boxes and folded tables and chairs, Grace found Bella. "How did you do?"

Bella made a so-so gesture with her hand. "Okay...one high score game, the rest mediocre. You win some, you lose some. Some of these seniors are crafty, aren't they?"

"That they are," Grace said, smiling.

She was about to ask about Tom when Bella said, "No news since they came off the ridge. They're following the river, so that's pretty easy riding. Try not to worry. He'll be home soon and will be very glad to see you."

Grace blanched. "Not sure about that after all I've put him through, but it will be good to have him safe."

Bella stared at her with kind eyes. "I know my brother, Grace. He's crazy about you in a way I've never seen with any woman."

"Night, Bella," she said, grabbing her jacket and departing along with the last of the players. *And even though I'm scared to death, I'm crazy about him too!*

CHAPTER 35

The pack trip returned late Friday afternoon. The Lodge vans sat ready to take them back to spa treatments, whirlpools, and saunas. Jeb, Brendan, and the three guides helped unload and assisted people down from their horses. Ben Senior gratefully accepted Jeb's arm as he dismounted. "Thanks, son. No matter how many days we do this on the trail, our bodies are ready for a hand at the end of it."

"Welcome home," Maggie said, hugging her husband for several minutes. "You're never going on a pack trip again."

He bent and kissed her forehead. "Hey, babe, am I glad to see you."

"I've got the ambulance standing by. Does the scorpion bite need medical attention?"

"I think he's fine, but I'd feel more confident if Chester checks him out. Can you call over there, then grab someone to take him into town?"

Sonny was slumped on a bench near the barn, Ursula standing nearby. "I'll take him."

Maggie nodded. "That'd be great. Hold on and I'll call Dr. Black, then get you a vehicle."

A few minutes later, with Ursula and Sonny on the way to town and the rest headed for the Lodge, a Volvo SUV flew into the lot and Leonora jumped out. Her husband was walking around the yard on stiff legs, chatting with people, and she hobbled to him, throwing herself into his arms.

"Ben Morgan, don't you ever do that to me again!"

"Hey, hey, honey, I'm fine. Had the time of my life."

"I'll just bet you did! And you," she said, pointing to her son. "I'll be speaking to you later! For now, I need to take this one back to the house. Your sister's at the hospital in labor. Harley's with her, and we're in charge of Charlotte. I want to get back and help Carm and also get your dad in a hot bath." She looked up at her husband. "Unless you'd rather go to the Spa for a treatment?"

"Home, darling. I hope our baby's okay."

"Pish tush, Ruthie's strong as an ox. Now, come on."

Maggie smiled, watching her in-laws walk to the SUV. "You're just lucky Ruthie went into labor this afternoon to distract her, or she'd be skinning you alive right now."

Ben laughed, holding her close and turning to Nick, Tom, and the others "You okay with unpacking all this? I'd like to take my wife home."

"Go," Tom said. "We've got it. Good job, boss."

"Thanks, guys," Ben said, arm around Maggie as they walked to her SUV parked in the barn lot.

An hour later, the horses had been fed and brushed. The camping gear was stowed in the barn until the following day when they'd wash and air the tents and bed rolls. Leftover food was put aside to be delivered to the local soup kitchen in the morning.

"Hey, guys, I'm gonna take off and let you youngins finish up, okay?" Tom said.

"No worries, Gramps," Nick called, even though the two men were the same age.

"I'll send the trailer for Echo is the morning," he said, waving as he headed for the truck. *Gramps indeed!*

∾

Unable to wait a minute longer, Grace punched in Tom's number.

"Hey." He answered on the first ring. "Good to hear from you."

"I'm sorry to interrupt," she said. "I was just checking to see if you're okay."

"Just driving in my driveway. I'm ready for a shower and a real bed, but otherwise, I'm doing great. How are you?"

"Better... I'm... Well, I'm doing better every day. I'll tell you about it when I see you."

"I like the sound of that. I'd love to see you."

"You're probably busy after being away?"

"Kind of. My days are going to be crazy, but I might be able to grab a bite to eat at night tomorrow or Saturday?"

"That's okay. I'm kind of busy Friday and Saturday," she lied. "I was thinking I might come out to see Dusty Sunday?"

"Of course. What time were you thinking?"

"Two? Two-ish?"

"Sounds good. I'll look forward to it."

"Me too. Well, I'll let you go. I'm glad you're home safe."

"Grace, I'm so glad to hear your voice. I've missed you," he said softly.

Tears sprang to her eyes. "Me too, you," she said. "See you Sunday, then."

"Yup, take care."

"You too."

She clicked off and began sobbing from relief and happiness. The sound of his deep, calming voice gave her the first comfort she'd experienced in several weeks. *Missing him doesn't even come close to how I've been feeling!* she thought as she stirred the stew she'd made for dinner.

CHAPTER 36

Life was a blur at Valley Stables upon Tom's return. In addition to the daily work of the stables, the community was celebrating the birth of Harley and Ruthie's daughter Penelope, or "Pickles," as they had decided to call her. The nickname was Harley's idea since his wife had craved pickles throughout her pregnancy and had sent him out repeatedly, at all hours, to find a certain kind, usually Carmela's from the Big House storeroom. Willow took a week off from college to come home and help with her new sister and Charlotte.

"Charlotte blows hot and cold," Harley told Tom in response to Tom asking how the toddler was adjusting to her baby sister. "One minute she's hugging the baby, next she's pressing down on poor Pickles's soft spot."

The two men sat outside the lower barn sharing a beer Friday night.

Tom laughed. "Legendary wrangler Harley Langdon sharing a home with four women. Who could have predicted that?"

"Why do you think I'm hiding out down here?" his boss asked, grinning. "Fortunately, I'm flexible."

"You're also an incredibly lucky man. Haven't met Pickles, but your other three women are the best."

"Yeah, they are. After a lifetime of dancing around the obvious, I'm very lucky that Ruthie and I finally got together. By the way, how are you doing in that department?"

Tom shrugged, giving him a wry smile. "We talked on the phone. That's a start."

"Yeah? Ruthie says she's been working hard to heal—therapists and all. Poor kid."

"Have you heard anything from Boone's office about the guy?"

"All I know is they sent him up to Florence. With any luck, Wilbur's testimony will be enough if the case goes to trial."

"Bastard," Tom muttered as Whip came by leading the last of the mustangs into the barn.

"Hey, how's it going?" Harley asked.

"Good. Ghost is still skittish, and he goes after Rusty whenever the Paint goes near the fence."

Harley shook his head. "We need to start working with him, or get rid of him. He spooks the others, so it's hard to work with them."

"I'll start next week," Tom said. "Was intending to make him my project till the pack trip came up."

"Dusty misses Grace too," Whip said. "Too bad she gave up on him."

"She hasn't. She asked if she could come over Sunday afternoon."

"Good news," Harley said as he stood. "Now, time for me to head home. See you all tomorrow."

Tom headed into the barn to help with feeding. "I'll take care of Ghost," he called to the three others, who were carrying buckets and curry brushes. They'd gotten the mares to accept a light brushing and Rusty too. So far, Ghost wouldn't let anyone near him and Dusty wasn't comfortable with anyone except Grace, who had not yet attempted to brush him.

Tom chided himself, as he'd been doing all day. *Never should have gone on that stupid trip at a time like this*, he thought, grabbing a pail of food. He headed for the white stallion's stall at the far end of the barn, separated from the others.

"Hey, Dusty," he said as he passed the Kiger's stall. "She's coming Sunday, so things are looking up."

SUNDAY MORNING, MAGGIE AND BEN DECIDED TO BRING THE KIDS TO Valley Stables. She packed a picnic, and they spread a quilt on the grass near one of the oval thoroughbred tracks. "Leo's looking good," Ben said to Tom as they watched Rupert circling the track. Harley stood at the fence timing them as Alice, the other jockey, adjusted Stella's saddle.

Tom nodded. "Gonna put Alice's nose out of joint when Leo reaches his full potential. He's the stronger, more consistent competitor."

"Mama, can we walk down and see the new horses?" Emma asked.

"Not without Dad or me," her mother replied. "Ben, what do you think?"

"I'd really like to watch this, babe. You okay to take 'em down?"

"Of course." Maggie struggled to her feet with Tom's assistance.

"I'll drive you down, then come back," Ben said.

"You'll do nothing of the sort. It's a beautiful day, and a short walk will do me good. Come on, kids."

As Maggie headed down the hill, Tom and Ben came to stand beside Harley. "Hey, buddy," Ben said.

"Hey," Harley said, grinning. "Come to watch World War Three?"

When Maggie and the kids reached the paddock, they spied Grace walking up from the barn. "Hi, Maggie, hi, kids!" she called.

"Hi, yourself," Maggie said. "Are you here to work with the Kiger?"

Grace nodded. "Visit might be more accurate. I kind of left him in the lurch the last time I was here."

As Ben the third raced back and forth along the fence, Whip joined them. "Hey, Benny the bee, no running or yelling, or you'll scare the new ponies." He turned to Grace. "Hey, you here to see Dusty?"

"Yes," she said, shyly since the handsome wrangler had witnessed their previous encounter. "Sorry for the last time. It wasn't fair to you or Dusty. How's he been doing?"

"Pretty good."

As they chatted, the Kiger approached, whinnying softly until he was nose to nose with Grace.

"Hey, sweetie," she said, petting him.

"Wow, that's amazing," Maggie said. "He's a beauty, isn't he?"

Grace looked over at Nick. "What do you think? Do I dare go in with him?"

"The boss told me if you do, I have to go with you."

"Okay if we try?" she said.

"Your call." He glanced over at Maggie. "Ms. Morgan, you feeling okay?"

"Just a small cramp. The joys of late-stage pregnancy," Maggie replied.

Grace observed her and agreed with Whip's concern. White as a sheet and sweating despite a cool breeze, Maggie gripped the fence. "Maggie, want us to find you a chair?"

"Absolutely not. I'm fine, really."

Whip opened the gate. "Okay, we can give it a try, but it would be helpful if the kids could settle down a little." He directed his remarks to little Ben since Emma was quietly observing at her mother's side.

"Of course," Maggie said. "Baby, will you get your brother? I have treats in my pocket. They might keep him quiet for a short time anyway."

Emma ran off to grab her brother, and Grace and Whip stepped inside the gate, closing it behind them. Dusty was alone in the round yard. Tom had moved the other three to the small paddock near the barn, and Ghost was in the largest enclosure adjacent to Dusty. "We've been moving them around, experimenting," he said.

"Ghost harasses the Paint constantly, so this keeps him farther away."

Dusty came right up to them, ignoring Whip as he nuzzled against her.

"Aww," she said softly. "I've missed you so much."

As she walked and talked to Dusty, Grace's gaze wandered. She wondered if they'd even see Tom with everything going on up the hill. Finally, he appeared just as Bennie broke free of his mother and sister and began running the fence line again.

Tom exchanged looks with Grace, smiling, then scooping up the child. "Hey, partner, we don't want to spook ole Dusty, do we?" As he held the wriggling child, Maggie screamed.

"My water's broken!"

As her mother doubled over in obvious pain, Emma watched, eyes wild and frightened. "Mommy, Mommy, what's wrong?"

"Looks like your mom's gonna have the baby soon," Tom said as he ran to Maggie's side, Ben in his arms. He turned to the two in the paddock. "Come on out of there now. Whip, run up and get Ben. He's at the track with Harley. Grace, can you and Emma handle this guy?"

Grace nodded. "Of course."

"Call the ambulance. Bella's home. I'll have her take a look." He grabbed his cell and called his sister, then looked over at Maggie.

She was panting, white-knuckled as she gripped the fence rail. "Oh, oh, oh!" she moaned.

Tom bent over her. "Think you can put your arms around my neck?" She nodded, and he swooped her into his arms and walked down to the barn. As they reached the door, Bella came flying down the hill from the house, medical bag in her hand.

"Lay her down here," Bella said, indicating a pile of hay just inside the barn door. After a quick examination, she looked up at Tom.

"We've called the ambulance, but it's at least twenty minutes away," he said.

"She won't make it," Bella said as they spied Ben in one of the farm utility carts, racing down the hill. "We need to get her to a bed. That cart will help."

Ben looked at his children, standing with Grace, her arms around their shoulders. "I've called my parents. Someone'll be here soon for the kids. Where's the ambulance?"

"Too far away," Bella said. "She's gonna have this baby now. We need to get her up to the house and onto a bed, quick."

Tom and Ben lifted Maggie into the cart, and they headed toward the house. Grace and the kids followed on foot. Just as they reached Tom's porch, the elder Morgans drove in.

Leonora leapt from the SUV and hobbled over to meet Grace and her grandchildren. "How is she?"

"About to give birth," Grace replied. "Bella didn't think they'd make it to the hospital."

"Oh Lord, here we go again! Hello, chickens," she said, turning her attention to her grandchildren as Ben reached the group. Grace noticed that he walked rather stiffly, and she wondered if it was due to his recent trail riding.

"Ben will take the kids to the Big House, and I'll stay," Leonora said.

Her husband put a hand on her shoulder. "We will both take the kids, darlin'. They're all set here, and they'll call us with any news. Ready to go?" he asked, reaching out to Emma and Ben.

"But—" she said, looking from the kids to Ben to Grace.

"Come on, Nora. Kids, let's get you back to the Big House. Carmela's just made a batch of cookies."

"I want to stay with Mommy," Emma said, burying her face in her grandfather's arms. They had a special relationship, and it was rare that he ever said no to her.

Ben looked up at Grace, and she smiled. "I'll stay with her, I promise."

"That's all I needed to hear. Come on, son." He lifted Bennie into his strong arms. "Grandma and I will take you back for some of those cookies."

As the three departed, Grace and Emma headed into the house.

They heard cries from the back, and Tom emerged from a hallway off the living room. "She's in my bedroom. Doin' just fine," he said, smiling at Emma before meeting Grace's eyes. "How are you doing?"

"Okay, good to see you."

"You too," he said, aching to put his arms around her. His beautiful Grace looked impossibly thin and fragile, as if she'd lost twenty pounds off her already slender frame. *Oh, my love*, he mused.

As the three of them stood in the living room, Maggie's screams pierced the silence.

CHAPTER 37

"I want to see Mommy," Emma said, pulling away from Grace.

Grace looked at the ten-year-old, then up at Tom. "Maybe Tom could check with your dad to see if it's okay?"

Tom nodded, disappearing down the hall. He returned shortly to say, "Your dad says yes, but asked that Grace stay with you just in case." He didn't elaborate on the "just in case" comment, but Grace understood. Should Maggie get into trouble, she would be responsible for whisking Emma out until the crisis was over.

When they entered the room, Ben was in the bed, behind his wife. His back against the headboard, he laid Maggie's against him as he cradled her, mopping her brow. Maggie looked almost peaceful as she rested between contractions.

"Hey, sweetie," Ben said. "Mommy's doing great. You hang back there with Grace."

"Hi, baby," Maggie said, her voice weak and hoarse as she held out her hand.

"Oh, Mommy, Mommy!" Emma cried, running to the bed, grasping her mother's hand, and burying her face in the bedclothes.

"Okay, Maggie," Bella said from her position at the foot of the bed. "With this next contraction, I want you to push. You ready?"

Maggie nodded, her teeth gritted as the next contraction seized her.

Ben exchanged looks with Grace. "Okay, sweet pea, Mommy needs to concentrate now, so you stand back a little way with Grace."

Grace guided the child back a step, but Maggie refused let go of Emma's hand. "She's fine, Ben!" she cried as the contraction crested and she groaned, then pushed with all her might.

"Good girl," Ben said, gently stroking her belly with one hand, smoothing back locks of her hair with the other. "You're almost there, babe."

Will I ever experience that kind of love? Grace thought, watching in awe at his loving attentions. Although in pain, Maggie leaned back, clearly comforted in the cradle of his embrace.

"The head is out," Bella said. "You're doing great, Maggie. One more big push now!"

As the baby emerged, Bella reached out to cradle her. "You have a beautiful baby girl," she said, wrapping the infant in a towel and handing her to Maggie.

"A girl!" Emma shouted. "It's a girl, Mommy!"

Misty-eyed, Grace watched as the little family welcomed the tiny baby into their world. Ben's arms circled all three of his loved ones, his face wet with tears. "You did good, babe. I love you so much!"

A few minutes later, Grace stepped out as Bella ministered to Maggie, and Ben and Emma took turns holding the baby. She found Tom in the kitchen pacing back and forth. "How are they? I heard a baby cry."

"They're perfect. It's a girl."

"Has she got a name?"

"I didn't hear one," she said, suddenly feeling weak-kneed, her legs like noodles.

"I'm... I'm feeling kind of dizzy."

Tom crossed the distance between them and caught her up in his arms. "Here, come sit," he said, leading her to a soft chair in the living room. "Can I get you something? Water? Juice? Something stronger?"

"Maybe some water, thanks," she said, giving him a wan smile.

When he returned, she was feeling better, and a few sips of water seemed to do the trick. "It was so amazing," she said. "I've never seen anything like it. Ben was so loving, and Maggie was incredible."

Afraid he'd spook her, Tom wasn't sure how to respond, so he knelt by her side, holding her hand. Finally, Grace placed the water glass on a nearby table. "I should probably go."

"Want me to drive you? I can have Whip or one of the guys follow in your truck."

"No, I'm fine, really." She patted his hand, then stood just as Chester Black came through the front door. "I'll leave you, then," she said, nodding to the doctor on her way out.

Tom wanted to walk her down to the barn, but Chester was already peppering him with questions, and by the time he'd answered him, then led him back to the bedroom, Grace was out of sight. A few minutes later, he spied her truck heading up the hill to the main drive. *A start*, he mused, waving.

CHAPTER 38

Wednesday afternoon, Grace arrived at the farm to find Greg Patterson mucking out stalls, but no one else around. "Hey, Grace," he called as she walked through the barn. "You here to see Tom or work with Dusty?"

"Both, I guess. Are you the only one here?" She smiled at the young cowboy as he pushed his hat back, revealing a line of dirt across his tanned forehead, his dark curly hair covered with dust.

"Tom had to go up to the stables for some emergency. Whip too. Said to tell you he'll be back soon. Also said for you to stay out of the round yard until he gets back. We've been having a lot of trouble with Ghost. He unsettles the other horses, even Dusty, who's not afraid of anything. Ordinarily, I'd be happy to come out with you, but I gotta get to these last four stalls before I head up to help on the hill. "

"No worries. You get back to it. I promise I'll visit with Dusty behind the fence."

"'Kay. He's in the round yard."

Adjacent to the large paddock, the round yard was only used for training. The Kiger stood alone, watching her every move as she approached. Fifteen minutes later, she spied Tom's truck coming down the drive. The past few weeks had been unusually dry in the moist valley, so a cloud of dust trailed after the truck. Tom waved, then disappeared into the barn, emerging several minutes later.

"Hey," he said, coming to stand by her. He patted her shoulder lightly.

"Hi. Looks like you're super busy around here today. Should I come back another time? I don't want to take you away from your work."

"Nowhere I'd rather be," he said. "They had an issue up the hill, but I left Kitteridge to deal with it."

"Can I go in?" she asked as she continued to pet Dusty.

"We'll go in, but I'll hang back as he's more comfortable with you. I was thinking, if you're up for it, we could try to put a light blanket on him."

Her eyes registered fear for a second, then she said, "Of course. That'd be great."

"Okay, then, I'll get you two settled and then run to the barn for the blanket."

As Tom hung back, Grace moved to the center of the round yard. The Kiger followed her like a puppy, a huge, solidly built puppy. They worked together for a while, Grace directing him to a trot around the edge of the yard.

"He's looking really great," Tom said, "relaxed and comfortable. You can turn and let him come to you and rest while I run and get the blanket."

As soon as she let up with the voice commands, Grace turned her back on the horse as Nick had taught her, and sure enough, Dusty came right to her, his massive head resting on her shoulder. "Good boy," she whispered, reaching back to pet him as she leaned against him. After all the years of fearing horses, she realized that she totally trusted the creature at her side. Loved him and felt comforted by his presence.

As they stood waiting for Tom to return with the blanket, a stirring and snorting from the next paddock cause her to turn. Ghost, the magnificent yet terrifying white stallion, was pacing, watching their every move. "Too bad he isn't more like you," she said nuzzling against the Kiger.

As she watched, the stallion retreated, and she assumed he'd gotten bored and had turned his attention elsewhere. Suddenly, to her horror, Ghost reared up with an ear-splitting squeal and headed straight for the paddock fence. He cleared it easily and galloped the short distance to the round yard.

Dusty snorted, placing his body between Grace and the angry stallion. Frozen to the spot, Grace screamed, "Tom! Help!" just as the stallion cleared the much lower round yard fence. The two horses clashed, hooves flying just as Tom raced up and cleared the fence in fluid jump. Greg was right behind him. He scaled the fence and followed his boss, a leather training stick in one hand. Tom reached Grace, took hold of her arm, and pulled her away, almost flinging her into Greg's arms. "Get her out of here, now!" he said, turning back to the horses.

Dusty held his ground, but the white stallion was several hands taller, and his hooves and his teeth had already left angry open wounds. Tom confronted the stallion, waving his arms and the blanket. Ghost's eyes were wild with fright as he reared again, a black hoof striking Tom to the ground, knocking him out.

"Tom!" she screamed from behind the fence. "Stay put Grace!" Whip yelled, joining Greg as they cautiously approached the two horses. Dusty had placed himself between Tom and the stallion shielding him as he snorted and reared, waiting for the next attack.

As Grace watched in horror, Tom came to and attempted to stand up. The white stallion was a short distance away, pacing and kicking out with his rear hooves, fetlocks flying.

Whip and Greg each took one of their boss's shoulders and dragged him toward the gate. Once outside, they set him on the grass, and Grace knelt, cradling him. Tom looked dazed and confused, but was clear enough to say, "See if you can get a rope around the stallion and get Dusty out of there. If you don't, Ghost'll kill him."

As the men ran back into the round yard, Tom looked up at Grace, giving her a loopy smile. "I'm glad you're safe," he said, then passed out again. Grace pulled her phone from her pocket and called Bella, who was on her way home from work. "I'll be there in ten minutes, sooner if I can," she said. "Keep him awake!"

Miraculously, the two men, aided by several others who had come down to begin the evening feedings, managed to lasso the white stallion and tie him to the fence. As soon as Ghost was subdued, Dusty left the fray and trotted to the fence near where Grace held Tom.

"Good boy," she said, wishing she could go to him, but not daring to leave Tom.

Bella arrived shortly before the ambulance. Tom was awake again, but fuzzy. After looking him over, she declared, "You're going to the hospital, big brother. That's a pretty nasty bump."

"Not necessary," he said, trying to sit up, then slumping back against Grace.

"You okay, Grace?" Bella asked as the ambulance's siren heralded its arrival.

"Yes, I'm fine. He saved my life," she said, tears in her eyes.

Not quite successful in hiding her fear, Bella helped the EMTs load her brother on a stretcher. As they prepared to go, she looked at Grace with kind eyes. "He's going to be fine. Looks like a concussion. I'll ride with him."

"Can I follow shortly?"

"Of course. See you there."

As they headed off, she went to Dusty, running her hands over his back, now pocked with bites and hoof marks. "My poor, brave Dusty," she said softly as she buried her tear-streaked face in his mane. The horse nickered softly, nuzzling against her.

"You go on. We'll take care of him," Whip said.

Grace hesitated, but with a pat on Dusty's nose, she turned to Whip. "I'll come back and check on him later, if that's okay?"

Whip nodded. "He'll be in his stall. We'll try to clean him up, but if he's agitated, your presence might help."

With that, Grace ran to her car and tore out of the yard.

CHAPTER 39

Grace found Bella and Tom in the emergency room. He lay on a cot in a small cubicle, his sister seated beside him.

"Hey," Tom said, giving her a crooked smile.

"How are you feeling?" Grace asked, looking from brother to sister.

Bella stood. "Perfect timing. They've already stitched up that hard head of his—just two stitches—and I can take him home in a bit."

"Is that safe?"

"Mild concussion. He's been alert and responsive the whole time." Bella waved to her now-vacant chair. "Please sit. I've got to fill out his discharge papers, and I'll be back."

When his sister whisked out of the cubicle, sliding the curtain closed behind her, Grace reached out and took his hand. "Are you sure you're okay? I mean, they would probably keep you for observation if you insisted."

"No way." He smiled, squeezing her hand. "I'm fine, really. As my sister says, I have a hard head."

"Some pair we are," Grace said, returning his smile. "Twin concussions. What disaster's coming next?"

"Doesn't matter at all if I'm with you."

"Oh, Tom, I'm so sorry."

"For what?"

"For pushing you away. For turning into a frozen, nasty mess. For repelling all your kindness and love."

"Grace McGraw, you have nothing—I mean nothing—to be sorry for. Besides, you're here now. That's all that matters."

She stood. "Can I hug you?"

Tom opened his arms. "What do you think?"

She scooted up beside him on the cot as he took her in his arms. *Home*, she sighed, breathing in his scent, her body warm for the first time since the attack. *I love you, Tom Jacobi*, she thought, and hoped he sensed it, even if she didn't speak the words aloud.

As they waited for Bella, Grace told him about her therapy and the progress she'd made. As she completed her description, he said, "I'm glad for you, baby. Glad you're healing and glad to have you in my arms."

"Me too. When I saw Ghost's hoof coming down on you, I died inside. I thought we might lose you," she whispered, snuggling closer.

"Hard head, remember? So how's the hero of the hour doing? That Kiger saved both of our lives."

"Yes, he did. Whip was going to clean him up, and I thought I'd stop by the barn on my way home. Poor baby had a lot of cuts and bruises."

"Horse fights can be brutal. Did they manage to get Ghost under control?"

She nodded. "He was tied to the fence when I left."

"That's a problem we'll have to face soon," he said as Bella returned. "Maybe we'll drive down to the barn on our way home."

"Oh no you won't!" his sister said. "You're going right to bed, no arguments. Ready?"

Tom draped his arms over both women, and the three of them walked out together. At Bella's SUV, they paused, and Tom held out his arms. "Since I'm apparently not allowed to come to the barn, I'll say good night here."

Grace hugged him tightly, never wanting to let go. "I'll let you rest tonight and check in tomorrow, okay?"

"Sounds good. Night, baby," he whispered, finally letting her go and sliding into his seat.

Bella turned to her. "I'm taking the day off to keep an eye on him, but feel free to stop in anytime."

"Thanks." Grace hugged her, then stepped back. As she watched them drive away, she felt like her heart had been ripped from her chest.

~

IN A DAZE ALL DAY, GRACE DROVE OUT TO VALLEY STABLES. SHE stopped by Tom's, but Bella answered the door and said he was sleeping. "He'll kill me for not telling him you're here, but neither of us got much sleep last night."

"No worries," Grace said. "I wanted to stop by and say hi to Dusty. Then I'll head home to make my dad's dinner. Tell him I say hello."

"Will do," Bella said, closing the door quietly behind her.

When she arrived at the barn, they were bringing in the horses. Dusty was already in his stall, pacing restlessly. When he spied her, he whinnied in greeting, nickering softly as she approached. "Hey, boy," she said, rubbing his nose. "How's he doing?" she asked Whip, who was passing by, leading Rusty.

"Pretty good. He could use a brushing and more ointment on his cuts. You're the only one he'll let in there, I'm guessing. You comfortable in the stall?"

Grace shrugged. "He was okay last night, and he needs the ointment, right?"

"Boss'll probably kill us, but since he was fine last night, let's give it a try. I've never seen a wild horse bond with someone like he has with you. Let me get Rusty settled, and I'll bring the stuff."

Not surprisingly, Dusty was calm, snorting softly as Grace gave him a gentle brushing. Careful not to go near his wounds, she talked to him in soothing tones. He didn't seem to mind the ointment as she began to apply it to every gash and bite. Whip left them to see to the other horses, and a few minutes later, Greg came in with a bucket holding Dusty's dinner.

"You're doing great with him," he said. "He's tame as a kitten around you."

"He's a good boy," she said. "How's Ghost doing?"

"Harley made the decision to move him up the hill. They have two isolation stalls away from the main stables. That way, he's away from all the horses until they decide what to do about him."

"Poor thing. He looked so frightened," she said, patting Dusty's withers as she completed his dressings.

"Yeah. Some horses never adjust. Here, I'll take those," Greg said, taking the cloths and ointment from her.

"Thanks, Greg." A few more pats and she stepped out of the stall, saying a final good night to Dusty.

"Night, sweet boy," she whispered.

CHAPTER 40

Fridays were always busy at the store, and this week was no exception. Paul and Paulo were out on deliveries most of the day, while customers streamed into the store, keeping Grace and her father running around from early morning until closing. As she headed to the house to start dinner, Grace pulled out her phone to discover five missed calls from Tom. As she climbed the back steps, she called him. "Hi."

"Hi!" he replied.

"Tom, I'm so sorry. I'm just seeing your calls. It's been a crazy day at the store."

"No problem. It's been crazy over here too."

"Don't tell me you've been working?"

He chuckled, the deep, throaty laugh she adored. "Light chores, a few meetings, and lots of delegating. This 'take it easy' thing is driving me crazy."

"But it's really important."

"So I'm told."

"How are you feeling?" she asked, wishing they were snuggling in a private place, just the two of them.

"Monster headache, but otherwise fine. Doc said it should be fading soon."

"Well, take it easy, please. Did you need me for something?"

"Sorry for all the calls. Since I think about you constantly, there could have been hundreds more, but the reason I was calling was to see if you're free Sunday. Saturday, we're meeting with Nick Parker to decide what to do about Ghost, then I've got to be at the stables all day, so I was thinking about a picnic Sunday? Lunch or whenever you're free?"

"I'd love to."

Tom said he had a place in mind, so they decided on a time. Grace offered to pick him up, but he insisted he was fine and would pick her up as well as bring all the food. She insisted she would bring dessert, and they rung off.

THE STORE WAS HOPPING SATURDAY, BUT THE GUYS WERE BOTH working, so Grace left a little early to bring a gift to Ruthie and the baby. Grace was greeted at the door by an unfamiliar young woman who introduced herself as Paula, Willow's roommate. "I'm the backup babysitter and chef, although with all the food Mrs. Morgan keeps bringing over, no one will need to cook for six months. Come on in. They're all upstairs. Pickles is being well cared for by her big sisters so Ruthie can sometimes rest between feedings."

"That's good news," Grace said, smiling at the short, stocky young woman in tie-dyed overalls, T-shirt, and Birkenstocks, her curly black hair tucked under a bandana.

"You know your way up?"

"Yes, thanks," she said, climbing the stairs to the beautiful third-floor living room.

She found Ruthie reclining on the couch nursing Pickles while Willow and Charlotte played a game. A laundry basket filled with washed baby clothes sat beside them. Grace scooped up the basket and came to sit beside her friend. They chatted, and she folded.

"How are things with the hunky Mr. Jacobi?" Ruthie asked as Grace finally put the folded laundry aside.

"Better...good... We're going on a picnic tomorrow."

"Hmm... That sounds romantic. Where are you going?"

"He wouldn't say."

Ruthie grinned. "Definitely romantic."

"Did I hear romantic?" Harley said, stepping into the room.

Willow waved as Charlotte left their game and ran to him. "Daddy!"

Harley swung her up into his arms, kissing her chubby cheek. "Hey, princess!" He then turned his hundred-watt smile on his wife and Grace. "How are you ladies doing?"

"Great," Ruthie said. "I have the best helpers in the world, and Mom has delivered enough food to keep us till the Fourth of July."

"That's Leonora," he said, stooping to kiss her. "Saw Paula in the kitchen, and she's warming up a mountain of stuff. Grace, you want to join us?"

"Yes, please stay!" Ruthie said, grabbing her hand.

"Thanks. I wish I could, but I'm having dinner with my aunt. She has something she wishes to discuss, most likely my dad."

They chatted a few minutes longer, and then Grace said her goodbyes, wondering again what Gracie wanted.

As usual, the diner was packed when she arrived. "Where is your dad tonight, anyway?"

Gracie asked as she slipped into the booth she had reserved toward the back of the restaurant. She had a full staff of waitresses and kitchen help, and she had put Andy Garcia, her assistant, in charge of the cooking, telling her niece, "He has to learn the ropes someday."

"Dad's playing poker, which means I'll be scraping him off the kitchen floor later," Grace answered, giving her aunt a wry smile.

"Which is exactly what I wanted to talk to you about. You in the mood for trout? We got a bunch of fresh ones this afternoon, and I did the prep work, so they're gonna be great."

"I'd love trout," Grace said, sipping her wine, waiting for her aunt to begin.

Gracie waved her hand with two fingers up, catching Maria's attention. When the waitress looked up, her boss mouthed the word trout, then turned back to her niece. "Order's in. Now, how are things going at your place?"

They chatted for a while about day-to-day life, skirting the subject of her father's drinking. Finally, Gracie said, "Right, well, then. I wanted to talk to you because it's clear to me that my stupid brother's behavior prevents you from having a life of your own." Gracie paused, suddenly discovering a small crust of bread stuck in her curly hair.

"But—"

"Let me finish, sweetie. You've taken extraordinary care of him since your mama died. That was okay for a while, but now you have a chance at real happiness with Mr. Jacobi, and I'm not having my brother spoil it."

"He won't. I can—"

"No, I can. You know you're the daughter I never had, Grace. I love you and my brother, and it's time for me to do my part. Aside from my waste-of-time ex-husband, who doesn't count, I have no other family. I've been training Andy to take over more so I can take a day off now and then."

"That's great news," her niece said. "You certainly deserve it."

"We'll see," Gracie said, nodding to Maria as she set their dinners before them and disappeared. "Anyway, I want you to know that if you and Tom form a deeper attachment, do not think about your father's needs. I'll see to them. He can move into my place, or I'll sell my bungalow and move into your house. Either way, I'll keep him in line so you don't have to worry about him anymore. I might even rope one of your siblings into helping me."

"Yeah, right," Grace said, smiling. "Juls is the only one who ever comes because she doesn't have a family, but I can't see her leaving Denver, her job, and Ewan behind. And Mac and Kathy are much too involved in work and their families."

"With the right enticement, you never know," Gracie said, smiling. "I'm serious, sweetie. I want you to know my intentions just in case."

"Just in case what?"

Her aunt's eyes twinkled with mischief. "Let's eat. Looks like Andy didn't make too much of a mess of this trout."

CHAPTER 41

Sunday was a glorious sunny day, clearer and warmer than they'd had in months. Tom picked her up shortly after noon. She jumped in, placing a tin of cookies from the café in the backseat next to his cooler. She had dressed in comfortable jeans, sneakers, and her favorite cotton sweater, a sage green that deepened her eyes from hazel to soft green. He was also in jeans, sport shirt and hiking shoes rather than his usual cowboy boots.

"You look amazing as always," he said, leaning over to hug her.

"You too," she said, feeling the heat rise in her cheeks at his nearness. "Where are we going?"

"Not far," he replied, heading out of town, turning south on the Gila Highway, a misnomer as the two-lane road was no super highway. "Not sure I've told you, but when I first came to town, I rented a cabin south of town till the bunkhouses were completed. I did some hiking in my free time and found a cool place. It's called Morgan's Pond. I don't think it's on the ranch property, so the name may not have anything to do with *the Morgans*. I've never asked. Have you ever been there?"

She shook her head. "I've lived here my whole life and have never heard of it."

Tom grinned. "That's what I was hoping. This way, I can give you a surprise."

A mile later, he turned off the Gila onto a dirt road. Near the end, they passed a small cabin. "Chez Jacobi for six months," he said as he drove on, the road becoming more and more rutted and muddy. Finally, he pulled over and parked in a small clearing, then jumped out and grabbed the cooler and a blanket.

"It's just a short walk. Promise. Want to put your tin in the cooler? There's room."

"That's okay. I'll carry it," she said, placing the tin on the hood of the truck and tying a light jacket around her waist.

The cooler's strap over his shoulder, he held out his other hand. "Shall we?" Her touch sent his libido through the roof. Tom took a deep breath. *Steady, boy, go slow.*

After a short walk, they passed through a natural arbor, a small pond ahead of them, a profusion of wildflowers blooming around its edge. On the opposite side, several cranes and herons drank from the glassy water, sending tiny ripples outward. The birds gazed up at the newcomers, squawked, and took flight. An expanse of green grass that appeared to be freshly mown stretched from where they stood to the edge of the pond.

"What a beautiful place," she said, gazing around in wonder. "Does someone maintain it?"

"No, that's one of the cool things about it. I'm sure only a few people even know it exists. At least I've never seen anyone here. I think this grass is a variety that stays green and low to the ground. Amazing, huh? You pick the spot, and I'll lay down the blanket."

She walked into the middle of the clearing, spreading her arms wide. "How about right here?"

He spread the blanket, and they unpacked the food, sipping iced tea as they each chose half a chicken salad sandwich, made by Tom that morning.

"Delicious," she said, smiling shyly.

"Glad you like it. There's a short hike up to another open spot, if you'd like to see it after lunch?"

"If I forget to tell you later, this is the loveliest gift you could give me after the past few weeks."

"You deserve lovely gifts every day," he said, reaching over to touch her soft cheek. "I've never brought anyone here. It's a sacred place to me."

Grace set down her sandwich. "Then it will be sacred to me from this moment on. I love you, Tom. I don't care if it's too forward or too soon because we haven't known each other very long. I don't expect for you to say the same, but I wanted you to know my feelings after all the hurt and confusion I've caused you lately."

"My beautiful Grace. Feel the same? I love you beyond all reason. I've never felt this way about another human being. No matter what happens, my heart is and always will be yours.

"I'd marry you tomorrow, but I won't ever rush you. All I want is to show you every moment of every day how much I adore you. If you let me, I intend make it my life's most essential work to make you happy."

"Tomorrow would be just fine," she said softly.

"We can take it as slow as you want, let you continue with your therapy and... Did you just say tomorrow would be fine?"

She smiled, pushing her lunch things aside and throwing herself into his arms. "Yes... Yes, I did! Tomorrow, next week, next month, whenever you want!"

"I wonder if the town justice of the peace is open on Sundays," he said as he pulled her closer, lips finding hers, kissing her deeply, their tongues finding each other in a sensuous dance. Clothes were soon discarded, their hands and lips exploring each other, desperate to come together in delicious harmony.

As he gently spread her legs, Tom said, "Are you sure, my sweet girl?"

She nodded, pulling him closer.

"If it's too soon, we can wait."

"Only one way to find out," she purred, arching up to urge him into her warm depths.

"I love you so much, baby," he said, grasping her ass as he entered her. *Home.*

"I love you too," she whispered as they came together, taking each other to the moon and back.

As they lay sated, the sun warming their moist bodies, Tom kissed her softly on her neck, then lips. Finally, he rose on one elbow. "I'm sorry, I don't have a ring because I never thought in a million years that you'd say yes, but we can go to the jewelers so you can pick one out."

"I don't need a ring."

"Yes, you do. But now, it's important that I ask you something directly. My beautiful Grace, will you make me the happiest man on earth and marry me?"

"Yes, yes, yes, Tom, I will, whenever you want, wherever you want, with all my heart."

Updates about future releases, please visit my AUTHOR WEBSITE and sign up for my Newsletter and Follow me on BookBub!

Read on for sample chapters of Morgan's Run book thirteen— *Bella's Touch!"*

BELLA'S TOUCH

Chapter 1

"Hey, aren't you working today?" Tom Jacobi asked, observing his sister in jeans and a work shirt pulling on her riding boots.

The remains of her breakfast on the table, Bella looked up, smiling as she reached for her coffee mug. "Morning. I have the night shift tonight, so I'm not going in till noon. I thought I'd take a ride this morning."

"Alone?"

She rolled her eyes, brushing a strand of dark brown hair from her cheek. "I've gone a bunch of times with you. I know the trail."

"No one's riding alone right now with the mountain lion sightings. Ranch rules. Guy was attacked last week."

"Okay, then I'll ride around the ranch, then take some laps on one of the tracks."

"Not today you won't. We've got time trials this morning, which is why I can't go with you." Tom lived and worked at Valley Stables, a vast property north of the town of Saguaro Valley. The dream of two wealthy friends, the ranch trained and raced prize thoroughbreds and also ran a small wild horses rescue program. Tom was the assistant manager of both operations, and as such, lived in a beautiful farmhouse halfway between the thoroughbred stables and the barn that housed the wild horses and stable horses, several corrals and round pens behind it.

Hands on hips, Bella said, "Tommy, look at me. I'm ready to go. I only want to go out for an hour or so. Couldn't one of the guys go with me?"

"Not the stable crew, but I suppose I could spare someone at the barn. Grace is coming to work with Dusty in a bit, so she'll be around." Tom's fiancée, Grace McGraw, lived in town, but spent many days and some nights at the ranch. Even though Grace worked at her father's hardware store in town, she had bonded with one of the wild horses, a Kiger whom she had named Dusty. Thus, she spent most of her free time with Dusty and Tom. "And after your joy ride, you can give us an hour's work to make up for pulling one of my guys from his work."

"Deal!"

"I'll call Whip." Tom grabbed his phone and stepped out on the back deck, the western mountains stretched out in front of him. He returned shortly. "If you get down there pronto, Whip says he'll go with you. He's saddling two horses right now."

"Thanks, big brother," she said, caramel eyes sparkling as she gave him a hug.

Tom grinned. "Get out of here, and be careful."

Bella had moved from Montana to the Valley two months earlier and was living at the farmhouse with her brother. According to her, the arrangement was temporary, only until she got settled and found a place. Tom insisted that she could stay forever and secretly hoped she would. Bella was good company and a great cook. Then he and Grace announced their engagement and things changed. Bella told him she would begin immediately to look at condos in town and on the river. A wedding date had yet to be determined, and as far as Tom could tell, Bella had yet to go condo shopping.

A warm breeze blew through the yard as Bella headed down the hill. As she neared the beautiful newly built barn, she removed her work shirt and tied it around her waist. It was going to be a hot one. Gentle nickering and the scuffling of hooves sounded as she stepped into the cool, dark space, the smell of fresh hay all around her. She could see two horses saddled and tethered to a fence post just outside the door at the opposite end. Several men were leading other horses out to the fields and corrals, and she said hello as she passed by.

Greg Patterson emerged from one of the stalls leading a sturdy dun-colored horse. Like most of the wranglers, Greg was strong and lean, his curly dark hair stuffed under a worn Stetson. A real charmer, his brown eyes and good looks had caused many a Valley woman to swoon. So far, he remained unattached.

"Morning, Greg, morning, Dusty," Bella said as she came to pet the horse's broad, soft nose. Such a gesture would have been unthinkable two months ago for anyone but Grace.

"Hey, Bella. Whip's got your rides all set. He had to run up to the stables, but said he'd be back in five."

"Thanks. Can I help you with anything while I wait?"

"I think we're set, thanks. Only one still in the barn is Ghost, and it takes two of us to drag his sorry ass out."

Bella nodded and peeked into the last stall, separated by an empty space at the far end of the barn. The magnificent white stallion snorted and pawed as she passed by. One of five wild horses to come to Valley Stables several months ago, Ghost was the last to be gentled. Between Tom and Nick Parker, a horse whisperer who worked at Morgan's Run, they had managed to get a rope on him, and occasionally a blanket, but that was it. He still needed to be in a separate corral from the other horses, and he viewed Dusty, in particular, as his biggest rival.

"Don't go near him unless you want to get nipped. He's nasty," a voice said from behind her.

She turned to find Whip Kittredge, her brother's unofficial right-hand man, leaning against a stall door. "He's sure gorgeous." Bella smiled at the wrangler. *And so are you.* She followed the tall, laconic cowboy with shoulder-length blond hair, beard, and mustache, as he strolled toward her. Some people called Whip "Wild Bill Hickok," but Bella had seen photos of Bill Hickok, and the showman and folk hero had nothing on this guy. His smoky-gray eyes shimmered with warmth as he neared, craggy features aligned and perfect when he smiled. *Wild and woolly, but oh so sexy!*

"You ready?"

"Sure am." As he passed by, she realized too late that she'd been gawking. Whip stood beside Galahad, a stable horse from up the hill. A retired racehorse, Galahad had been bought for stud. Beside them, Whip's Appaloosa, Calico, waited patiently. "You brought Galahad down?"

"Yup. Boss's orders. He's a gentle ole guy."

"Yes, he is," Bella said, coming to scratch and pet the black thoroughbred who nickered and nudged her affectionately. "Galahad and I are old friends. But how'd you get him down here so quick?"

Whip smiled. "I delegated. One of the crew up there brought him down. They move fast."

"I guess so." She easily mounted the steady horse, settling herself in the saddle. As Whip adjusted her stirrups, she noticed the shotgun strapped to Calico's saddle. *Cougar defense,* she thought and suddenly felt guilty interrupting his work to babysit her. Mountain lion sightings were almost a daily occurrence now, which made her little joy ride a risk. "Thanks for doing this, Whip. I hope it's not going to make everyone's day tougher."

"Not at all. The guys'll just work faster and harder."

"That's what I mean! My brother says I owe you an hour's work when we get back."

"Lucky us," he said, effortlessly mounting his enormous black-and-white-spotted horse in one fluid motion. "Come on, buddy," he said, making sounds somewhere between a click and a kiss.

Chapter 2

In most places, the trail was wide enough for the two horses to be side by side. As they proceeded at a languid pace, they conversed about the weather, the ranch, and other innocuous subjects, each keenly aware of the other's nearness. From the moment his boss's sister had arrived, Whip had been smitten by the dark-haired beauty, with her soft caramel eyes and her intoxicating scent of bergamot and desert rose. Out of his league, he knew, but a guy could dream. When Maggie Morgan had gone into labor next to the corral several months earlier, he had marveled at Bella's gentleness and expertise as a midwife as she cared for the terrified woman. Bella was a healer, something sacred in his opinion.

Despite her dismissal of her riding prowess, Bella was an experienced horsewoman, comfortable and confident in the saddle. Galahad sensed her confidence and trotted along, unfazed as she shifted in the saddle and threw her head back in laughter. She had a deep, very sexy laugh.

As they rode, his eyes constantly scanned their surroundings. "You're looking for the cougars, aren't you?" she asked.

He grinned. "Cougars, javelinas, rattlesnakes, scorpions, you name it. Doesn't pay to relax your vigilance anywhere out here."

"Have you seen one? A lion, I mean?"

"Not here, but plenty back home."

"Which is?"

"Vancouver Island."

"British Columbia? You're Canadian, then?"

"Dual citizenship."

"Wow, I wouldn't have figured that," she said, gazing at him in surprise.

He shrugged. "Most everyone here is from somewhere else. Look at you and your brother."

"I guess."

A rustle in the nearby brush caught his attention, and Whip reined in Calico, reaching over for Galahad's bridle. "Whoa, boy."

As they watched, a group of six javelinas emerged from the brush and crossed the path. Since horses and riders were downwind, the poor-sighted creatures appeared to be unaware of their presence. Neither Galahad nor Calico made a sound. When the pig-sized peccaries disappeared, they continued.

"They are the funniest creatures, aren't they?" she said.

"Look like wild boars, act like wild boars, and don't much like people. They're also a favorite food of the mountain lion."

"Really?"

"Them and horses."

"Did you have javelina where you grew up?"

"Nope. Javelina like the heat."

They rode about ten minutes more before Whip turned toward a stream bordering the trail. "Let's stop and give 'em a drink,, then we'd better turn back," he said, slipping off Calico and letting the horse go to the water. He then came to help her down, his hands grasping her waist as she slid off.

Bella felt her face heat up and knew she was blushing. "Thanks," she said, stepping back.

He grinned. "No problem."

"So, Vancouver Island...that must've been a cool place to grow up."

He shrugged. "Probably not all that different from where you guys were. Montana's pretty spectacular."

Bella sat on a fallen log near him. "I've never been to Vancouver. What's it like?"

"Where we are, wild. My dad was a logger, but when the mill closed down, he opened an adventure tours company. It's pretty successful, actually. He wanted me to stay and work for him, but schlepping a bunch of touristas around isn't my idea of fun. I love horses. I knew I wanted to work on a ranch."

"So, your parents still live there?"

He nodded. "My parents and my sister. She works with Dad. My mom's a blogger, 'Gold River Belle.' I hear she's popular, but I don't follow her."

"What about other brothers and sisters?"

He stood abruptly. "You sure ask a lot of questions. We better get going. I have a ton of work to do."

Startled by the change in his tone and his brusque behavior, Bella observed the tight muscles in his back as he went to the horses, untying Galahad and whistling to Calico, who immediately came to his side.

"What's wrong?" she asked.

"Nothing. Just lost track of time. You ready?"

"Of course." She ignored his outstretched hand, grabbed hold of the pommel, and mounted Galahad without his assistance.

They rode back in silence, Bella admiring the scenery and trying to ignore the rude man riding ahead of her. When they neared the end of the trail, Valley Stables came into view. An exhibition was going on with horses from around the area, so the grassy parking lots near the tracks were full and spectators lined the fences. Whip skirted the tracks and led her behind the stables. As they passed the complex and headed down the hill, Tom spied them. He'd just emerged from showing the stables to a group of clients. Whip tipped his hat and his sister waved, but they didn't stop.

Hmm...what's the matter with those two? Tom thought, watching them. *Just as well.* He liked and respected Whip, but wasn't crazy about him becoming too chummy with his sister. He knew his assistant had a troubled past, but had never asked for details.

Outside the barn, Bella dismounted and turned to him. "Shall I groom him here or take him up to the stables?"

Whip pushed his hat back, scratching his forehead as he looked over at Galahad. "He'll stay here with us for the day, but one of the guys can do it after they finish the stalls."

"I owe you an hour's work, remember?"

"Not necessary, but thanks anyway."

"Well, I say it is!" she replied a bit more stridently than she intended. "I'll brush him down, put him out, and see if they need help with the stalls. That should keep me busy." With that, she turned on her heel and stomped off, leading Galahad into the barn. Once inside, she realized she had no idea where to get curry brushes, buckets, or water. Fortunately, she ran into Greg with a wheelbarrow of dirty hay.

"Hey, Greg, where should I cool Galahad down?"

Greg had a huge shit-eating grin on his face, and she wondered if he'd observed their little scene.

"You can use the stall at the end. All cleaned. There are brushes in a bucket. The hose is right there too."

"Thanks," she said, refusing to meet his gaze or look back in the direction she'd come.

An hour later, covered with hay and dust, Bella admired the three stalls she'd mucked out. Whip and Greg were nowhere to be seen, and the other two guys who'd been mucking alongside her had also disappeared. She paused, and the stillness of the barn enveloped her, the sweet smell of fresh hay comforting. After a few minutes, she stowed her pitchfork and headed up to the house for a shower.

Chapter 3

When Whip walked by the farmhouse, he noticed that Bella's old blue Highlander was gone. He realized he'd been a jerk, but the mention of siblings had touched a nerve and a part of his past that he wasn't prepared to open. He carried photos of Johnny and Ellie in his wallet and looked at them every morning and every night, but he sure as hell wasn't ready to talk about them.

Suddenly, he heard clip-clopping behind him and turned to find his boss on a tall gray Trakehner. Like Galahad, Blue had been bought for stud, to support their nascent dressage program. Blue had been a spirited, fierce competitor, but was now retired. Tom's favorite, most people assumed that the beautiful warm-blood belonged to him since they were always together.

Tom pulled up alongside him. "Good ride?"

"Nice morning for it."

Tom hopped off the horse and confronted him. "Not what I asked."

"All you're gonna get."

"What happened? Did she do something?"

"I'm just not great at babysitting novice riders."

Wrong answer. Tom's eyes narrowed. "You know damn well my sister's as competent a rider as you or me. Now what the hell happened?"

"Nothing, boss. I'm just having a crap morning."

"Because?"

"Because I'm me. Dark moods sometimes happen to me. Nothing to do with Bella."

"You want to talk about it?"

"Nope."

"Okay, fine." Tom mounted Blue. "But I'm here anytime. I'm no shrink, but I'm a pretty good listener."

"Thanks, boss."

Whip watched Tom ride off. "Shit, shit, shit," he muttered under his breath as he headed down the hill to say hello to Tom's fiancée, Grace, who was in the first of two round pens working with Dusty.

Bella arrived Valley Ob-Gyn twenty minutes before her first patient, Ruthie Morgan Langdon. One of her bosses, Dr. Marc Koenig, met her in the hall on her way to her office. "I smell horse," he said.

Bella's face dropped. "You're kidding! I took a long shower."

The tall, thin senior physician pushed sandy hair back from his forehead as he grinned at her. "Haven't you heard? I have super olfactory powers."

"No, I hadn't heard."

"Early morning ride?"

"Yup."

"Lucky you. I get out when I can, but my poor old Skip doesn't get near enough exercise these days."

"You have a horse?"

"Three, actually. My daughters ride competitively."

"Why did I not know this?"

He chuckled. "I like to think I have a few secrets."

"Where do you keep them? The horses, I mean."

"We board them at Morgan's Run now, but I'm on the waiting list at Valley Stables. My girls do dressage, and it would help to have them there for lessons and training. I mean, Maggie and her crew are terrific, but it's probably the logical next step. It was actually Maggie who suggested it."

"Did you know I live out there with my brother?"

"Yes, which is one of the reasons I've never mentioned it to you. Don't want any favors. I've brought up Maisie and Julie to stand on their own merits. It's something that was really important to their mom."

"Good for you. So important," Bella said, noticing that tears rimmed his blue eyes.

"Well... I won't keep you. Have a good day," he said, nodding as he turned away.

"Thanks. You too," she said.

"Hey, Jacobi," he called as she reached her office door. "Ignore the horse-smell comment. I actually like it."

She sat at her desk, pondering the interaction. *Was he flirting with me?* she wondered as she shuffled through the files for her afternoon appointments and powered up her computer on the cart beside the desk. She knew Marc had lost his wife, Bonnie, a year earlier after her long battle with cancer. She also knew he had kids, but not much else. For the two months she'd been at Valley Ob-Gyn, she'd kept her head down and worked hard, with little time for office gossip. After her last job in Montana, she preferred to keep her distance at work.

She'd become friends with Gretchen Sullivan, one of her fellow midwives, but otherwise, she socialized with townspeople. She'd joined Valley Chorus and the Scrabble Club, both of which Grace, her brother's fiancée, and Aria Firorelli, Spark Foster's chef, were regular attendees. Spark was one of the owners of Valley Stables. Grace and Tom encouraged her to come to Scrabble Night, and Aria had nagged until Bella agreed to try the chorus. She'd joined only a few weeks earlier, but she loved it.

Suzie Breen, one of the practice's physician assistants, popped her head in the door. "Hey, Bella, your one o'clock's here. I've put her in room two."

"Thanks, Suz. Be right there."

Bella stood, stretched, then grabbed Ruthie's file, tucking it under her arm. She draped her stethoscope around her shoulders and wheeled the computer cart out the door. *Feels like an appointment with the Queen Mother*, she thought as she knocked on the door of Examining Room Two. Wife of Tom's boss, Harley Langdon, Ruthie was here for her three-month post-birth checkup. Bella opened the door to find her patient perched at the end of the table, texting on her phone.

"Hi, Ruthie."

"Hi, Bella." Immediately, the petite redhead with freckles and pale blue eyes tossed her phone atop her pile of clothes lying in a jumble on a nearby chair. "Long time no see."

"Not too long," Bella said, smiling. "How are you?"

"Great. A little irritation at the site where I tore, but I've been taking lots of baths, and Harley's been real gentle."

"And how is your beautiful Pickles?"

"She's doing amazingly well. This is her first week at the Cottage, and they say she's settled in like a champ. My mom and Carmela are having baby withdrawal, but they'll get over it. Besides, there are plenty more babies for them to fuss over."

"You're so lucky to have the Cottage and so much support."

The Cottage was a day care and nursery built, staffed, and financed by the elder Morgans and their dear friend Spark Foster. Free and open to all children of their employees and, of course, their grandchildren, it was a lovely light-filled space with a well-equipped school and playground.

Most Morgan grandchildren spent their first months at the Big House with Granny Leonora and her housekeeper, Carmela. Carmela and her husband, Raoul, manager of the ranch's livestock, had never been blessed with children of their own, but had raised many Morgan offspring over the years. Penelope "Pickles" Langdon had been with her grandmother and Carmela, along with baby Cora, Maggie and Ben's third. Cora, who traveled between the Big House at Morgan's Run and Maggie's dad's in town, was still a few weeks away from joining the Cottage crew.

"We sure are."

Bella pulled the computer cart close and sat beside Ruthie. "Looks like all your vitals are great. Let's just take a quick peek and then we can chat in my office. Sound okay?"

Bella called Suzie in.

"Everything looks great," she said a few minutes later as she completed her examination and handed Ruthie her clothes. "I'll see you when you're ready, okay?"

Bella went to her office, typed up her notes from the exam and grabbed two waters from the cabinet. She had a rule—no computer work with the patient. Thus, she scheduled extra time to enter notes into the electronic files after the examination or before her next patient.

When Ruthie joined her a few minutes later, she pushed the computer cart aside and came around the desk to sit beside her on one of two office chairs. "So, you're in good shape and have healed well. I asked Suzie to grab samples of a cream you can put on your scar, and I'll phone a prescription into the pharmacy, just in case you want more. I'd suggest using it at least twice a day, but definitely after you wash and before and after intercourse."

"Thanks."

"They'll be at the desk when you check out. Now, what questions do you have for me?"

"Not many. Do I just return now to a yearly checkup."

"Yes, but if you have any concerns or questions, be sure to call or make an appointment before then. How's the nursing going?"

"You mean the pump-nurse, pump-nurse till my boobs feel like they're gonna fall off?"

"Are they sore?"

"No, they're fine. I use lanolin when needed. Pickles is a trooper. She latched on and has never let go. She transitions really well between bottle and breast, thank God."

"Good baby."

"So how are you settling in, Bella? Is Valley life suiting you?"

"I love it. Such beautiful country, and the people are so friendly. Most people, that is."

Antennae up, Ruthie eyed her. "Oh? Have you had trouble with someone?"

Bella smiled, waving her hands. "No, just a weird episode with Whip Kittredge this morning. My brother wouldn't let me ride alone, so he assigned Whip to babysit me."

"Smart, with all the cougar sightings lately. So what happened?"

"Everything was going great, then he just clammed up, turned stone cold, and stayed that way for the rest of the ride. It was very strange."

"No trigger?"

"We were talking about his family, and I asked about brothers and sisters, and *boom*, that was it."

"Hmm, I don't know Whip that well. I mean he's a great guy and I know Harley and Tom depend on him to keep the other guys in line, but I don't think anyone knows much about his past. I can ask Harley?"

"No, please don't. He was probably just in a bad mood. I certainly don't want to cause trouble."

"Okay, but I'll keep my radar up. By the way, we're having our Friday-night barbecue this week. I hope you and Tom are coming?"

"He hasn't mentioned it, but I'm sure we'll be there. Thanks."

They chatted for a few more minutes, then Ruthie said goodbye just as Suzie popped in to announce Bella's next patient. Bella decided to put Whip Kittredge and his moods out of her mind as she gathered her notes and headed in to greet a very pregnant Amy Barnes, daughter of Spark Foster. Her husband, Jeb, a wrangler working at Morgan's Run, was with her. Amy was due any minute.

Get Bella's Touch!

ALSO BY M. LEE PRESCOTT

Contemporary Romance

Morgan's Run Romances

Book 1: *Emma's Dream*

Book 2: *Lang's Return*

Book 3: *Jeb's Promise*

Book 4: *Rose's Choice*

Book 5: *Hope's Wonder*

Book 6: *Ruthie's Love*

Book 7: *Polly's Heart*

Book 8: *Kyle's Journey*

Book 9: *Gus' Home*

Book 10: *A Valley Christmas*

Book 11: *Aria's Song*

Book 12: *Tom's Ride*

Book 13: *Bella's Touch*

Morgan's Fire Romances

Book 1: *Lucy's Hearth*

Book 2: *Tim's Hands*

Book 3: *Pam's Garden*

Book 4: *Rich's Dilemma*

Book 5: *Lolly's Wish*

Book 6: *Greta's Goat*

Book 7: *A Horseshoe Crab Cove Christmas*

Well-Loved Romances

Widow's Island

Hestor's Way

Mystery

The Ricky Steele Mysteries

Book 1: *Prepped to Kill*

Book 2: *Gadfly*

Book 3: *Lost in Spindle City*

Book 4: *Poof!*

Also, featuring Ricky Steele:

Jigsaw

Roger and Bess Mysteries

Book 1: *A Friend of Silence*

Book 2: *In the Name of Silence*

Book 3: *The Silence of Memory*

Book 4: *Silencing the Pen*

Young Adult Historical Romance

Song of the Spirit

A NOTE FROM THE AUTHOR

I am so pleased to bring you Tom and Grace's love story, once again set in beautiful Saguaro Valley! After a scathing divorce, Tom is on the bench until he meets Grace, who struggles with heartaches of her own. This couple's love for one another and their sizzling, white-hot romance propel a story that includes encounters with scorpions and javelina, two family births, trail rides in the Arizona mountains, celebrations, handsome cowboys, beautiful women, and horses, of course!

Thank you so much for reading *Tom's Ride* and visiting this wonderful community with me. If you enjoyed the book and would be willing to write an Amazon review, I would be so grateful. If you would like to hear about future book releases, giveaways, and updates about my books, please visit my Author Website at *https://mleep-rescott.com/* to sign up for my newsletter and follow me on BookBub at *https://www.bookbub.com/search/authors?search=M.+Lee+Prescott*. I promise I will not share your address, nor will I flood you with emails.

Finally, this book has been revised, proofed, and edited many, many times, but if you spot a typo, please email me at *mleeprescott@gmail.com*, and I promise to fix it in the next edition.

Warm wishes,
M. Lee

ABOUT THE AUTHOR

M. Lee Prescott is the author of dozens of works of fiction for adults, young adults, and children, among them the Ricky Steele Mysteries, Roger and Bess Mysteries, and a number of stand-alone mysteries and romances. *Tom's Ride* is number twelve in her Morgan's Run contemporary romance series. New England hosts the spin-off romance series Morgan's Fire in the beautiful coastal village of Horseshoe Crab Cove. Her nonfiction titles explore contexts of young children's reading and writing and she has published numerous articles in the field of literacy education. Lee is professor emeritus from Wheaton College where she taught reading and writing pedagogy. Her research focuses on mindfulness and connections to reading and writing.

Lee has lived in southern California (loved those Laguna nights!), Chapel Hill, North Carolina, and various spots in Massachusetts and Rhode Island. Currently, she resides in Massachusetts on a beautiful river, where she canoes, swims, and watches an incredible variety of wildlife pass by. She is the mother of two grown sons and spends lots of time with them, their beautiful wives, and her beloved grandchildren. When not teaching or writing, Lee's passions revolve around family, yoga, swimming, sharing mindfulness with children and adults, and walking.

Lee loves to hear from readers. Email her at *mleeprescott@gmail.com*, and visit her website to hear the latest and sign up for her newsletters!

AUTHOR WEBPAGE AND NEWSLETTER SIGN-UP at *http://www.mleeprescott.com/*

FOLLOW ME ON BOOKBUB at *https://www.bookbub.com/search/authors?search=M.+Lee+Prescott*

If you have five minutes, please review this book!